# Desert Diya

Also by Adèle Ogiér Jones and published by Ginninderra Press

*Afghanistan – waiting for the bus*
*From the Edge of the Pacific*
*Beyond the Blackbird Field*

Adèle Ogiér Jones

# Desert Diya

*Desert Diya*
ISBN 978 1 74027 605 4
Copyright © Adèle Ogiér Jones 2010

First published 2010
Reprinted 2016

**GINNINDERRA PRESS**
PO Box 3461 Port Adelaide 5015
www.ginninderrapress.com.au

# Contents

# Prologue

## December 1999

A sharp tapping sound echoes through the early evening air – fingernail against metal repeating through the stillness. The first prayer call wakes her. The microphone is on.

She walks from the window to the door and the door to the window to vary the monotony.

*Time goes slowly here. In the desert, time is slow but the seasons refresh us. It is cool again and the rains have come again. How the birds love to play in the pools lying in the courtyard.*

*Each dusk I hear my birds, different birds when I walk by the wall. I see the birds in my mind, nestling close to the ground in little bushes which come to life after the early rains. Those trees in the corner are homes for these families who are flying to other countries. If only I could do the same. I want to join them on their paths.*

*I dreamed last night and in my dream I wept but it was not a sad dream – not until I woke and remembered where I was. Alim came to me – a real lover this time but he was gentle and he called his brother to me. It was Oscar. They both kissed me and I was happy in my dream. Then my child ran towards me and threw her arms around my legs. She was very little. It was Rita. Rita was my child. At that time I felt loved and wise. I seemed to understand many things but I could not remember what it was I knew so well.*

*The waters licked our feet. Crabs, red and gold, scurried across the black sand, glistening with silver flecks, each grain sparkling in the soft morning light. We did not hurt them.*

*In the distance, I could hear rumbling from the belly of a volcano. Black clouds rolled across the sky and a little blue bird which perched on a branch near my head sang and sang. When I woke, I could still hear it singing.*

Looking across the courtyard in the early morning light, she remembers the clicking of the looms as women wove red in black and purple in blue. Here there is little colour – sand and grey charcoal shadowed by the dawn rays. There is no light in the yard to brighten her spirits. Even the pigeons which would normally cheer her seem to carry bad news today.

Her dry hands each grasp a bar. She shakes the iron in frustration and leans against the windowsill. She knows people understand, or so they tell her, yet with a look in their eyes seem to blame her.

She shuts the diary, stands, looks through the small window to the courtyard and turns, ready to face them.

# The Journey

# 1

# January 2000

Long ago she had stopped crying except when she saw again her mother and father sitting on the other side of the table, reaching out to her – but this is a long way into our story, a story which could be true. Some would say it is, for many parts they have heard in some guise or other, in other places and over many years.

This story, Hana's story, was formed over a long period, told piece by piece, threads weaving in and out, a tapestry of light, disbelief and bitterness. This story takes place in a desert region but could just as well be set in cities, the tropics, amidst oil wealth and business riches. More like them have been told in other countries. Names have been changed for the sake of decency, though if we were to explain it at the outset, this is not a story about decency.

Her friends call her Hana, a compromise between the Hanan of her own community and the Annas, Annies and Anitas in the other part of her town. She had lived fifteen of her years in Cotabatu, a small town by Filipino standards, on the southern island of Mindanao. It is tropical but a paradise no longer and perhaps never was.

Hana's father, Janjalani, and his father, and his father before him were fishermen. Like many men in their area, he gave up this work when sea pirates and the country's army made the job so difficult that he could barely earn a wage. They were poor people but proud. They are Muslim, called Moros after the Moors of Spain. They dance a special dance and dress differently from other Filipinos, proud of the distinctive patterned cloth they twist into turbans, cloth woven by their women.

There were other groups in the family who were fighters. Hana knew that well, though they never spoke openly of this, not now as their people became targets of vigilance and violence. Many people in Mindanao had such men in their families. They are called freedom fighters or the Bangsa Moro Army – an arm of the Moro National Liberation Front. These men, for usually they are only men, fought against a government which opposed them, oppressed them and moved them away from their traditional lands along the coast.

There were others too. She knew of peasants from further inland – farming people who for decades, maybe centuries, had worked and survived in the tropical jungle. The army moved them too. 'Hamletisation' some called it. It was a nice, cosy word portraying images of peaceful villages where life went on as it had done for generations. This was far from the truth, though. Peasant farmers and their families were moved by force. They left their homes where once they had been one with the land. Some formed groups opposing the army and in return many were herded together so that the military had them where they could be observed. Under surveillance, they were monitored in their hamlets. They were controlled but the struggle went inland and was internalised, becoming more intense as other peasants and workers joined them.

This was development, they were told, as roads ate their way through farming and traditional lands and an older way of life was destroyed. The roads and the army intent on curtailing freedom blocked anything that seemed like a 'popular' movement.

These were some of the players in Mindanao – an island with many groups, many disenfranchised. Catholic peasants, Muslim fishermen and farmers on one side, and armies carrying out the dictates of governments long since reviled by Filipinos and international communities alike, on the other. Then there were some, fearing what they called radical elements, intent on taking control in shaky pockets of the country. Add to this rebel groups with tactics attracting media attention, bringing the fight for freedom into the limelight, and you see the environment Hana knew best.

'You write like a journalist. It doesn't seem like this day to day.'

'But isn't it true that your family and many families who live in Mindanao are suffering through dislocation?'

'Dislocation? That's what my family's history was all about. You talk about pirates. Some say smugglers. We had friends who sailed back and forth between Mindanao and Malaysia for as long as I can remember. That was their job. Some families lived in Mindanao. Some believed that this was really part of a Muslim land until one president took our land and gave it away and then moved farmers down here from Luzon. That's what people say.'

'So what was it like for you as a child?'

'We are a happy family. We don't have much. My father and mother both worked. My mother wanted to join the women's cooperative. There were Christian women in it too and even some sisters – you know – nuns who work with us. The co-op sold the weaving to tourists when they came to Davao and Zamboanga but they don't come much any more because it is dangerous and now the sisters send weaving to the cities and sometimes we sell it to merchants who take the cloth up north. It is special cloth. Many of the men wear it on their heads. That's how people recognise them.

'Our family is large, I suppose you'd say – eight children living. All of us went to school. I did well in primary school. I wanted to go on studying but it was difficult for us to get jobs in Mindanao and it was strange for us to become students anyway. It is not part of our custom. None of us has spent much time at school. In my family all the children went to the local *madrassah* because my father wanted us to have some religious training.

'I know all the families in our area. For several years when I was very young, we lived in a house built over the water. We built it high on posts so small fishing boats could pass easily underneath. We loved running along the planks which made bridges between the houses and it was fun climbing up and down the ladders to our boats. I was good at rowing when I was younger. My brothers taught me. Sometimes they used to take me fishing even though my mother complained. Once I was too old, I helped with the cooking or looked after my little brothers and sisters. I love the smell of dried fish and cooking *bilis* but I would rather have been out on the sea.'

She stops and gazes into the empty space opposite. 'But there's no chance of that now.'

She stops again and pulls her scarf further over her hair, rubbing hands along her arms as if she is cold. The naked bulb overhead highlights the pallor of her face and the deep lines running from her cheeks to the edge of her lips. These are etched from distress.

'Are you all right, Hana?'

She nods and looks up with eyes which make me feel clumsy for asking questions.

At other times there are things the girl remembers which comfort her – the sound of the water lapping against the poles holding up the wooden house, and the smell of the cigarettes her father smokes as he sits talking with the other men on those many evenings in the warm weather.

'But I didn't like the heavy rain which leaked inside our house in the wet season, especially if the wind blew hard. The sea was angry then,' angry, she knows, like her father could be, lashing out at everyone who gets in his way. Now, however, she mainly remembers the good things about him and the fact that he wants her back in his home no matter what they say.

'One of the happiest times for me was listening to the men praying. When we were little and living above the water, there was a small mosque there as well. It wasn't as beautiful or strong as mosques built on the land but it seemed part of us and the men would sit and chat there after dark sometimes. When we moved into stronger houses built on the land, I really missed my old life but I didn't complain because my mother always seemed sad about moving and I didn't want to hurt her more.

'Apart from the chores and homework, there was not a lot to do but life always seemed exciting when we were young. Even curfews didn't worry me because I always had to be home by nightfall. I wasn't as free as the Catholic girls and it didn't matter what time the boys got home, although when the fighting got bad my parents weren't happy if they were out late or if they were with the young men in town smoking and talking. My family never wanted trouble, not for the young ones anyway.'

'So how did you come to work here in the Gulf?'

'Because there's not much work in Mindanao and our country is poor as well, we have agencies which arrange work for men and women in different countries. Filipinas are hard-workers and we're honest. You just ask any people here if they want Filipinas working for them and they'll say yes every time.'

She grits her teeth to fight backs the tears, clenches her right fist, grinding it into her other palm over and over again. She had known of others who went to work overseas. It seemed a privilege for them in Mindanao to work in the Gulf and the new rich states in nearby east Asia. Here they were Muslims too and they ruled their own lands.

'Men and sometimes women would come around for a few weeks or even a few months every year. People would give them their names and tell them the type of work they would like. I talked to my parents many times about the people who went to work overseas. I didn't really think about going but we knew that people made a lot of money and sent cheques back to their family. Sometimes they would build a house or buy a shop with this money. Our friends opened a mechanic's workshop and fixed people's motorbikes and cars. Jeepneys would come there because the boys in the family did such a good job. They all worked hard but the money from overseas really helped a lot.

'I remember one girl I met at school who had a brother working in the Gulf. It seemed really mysterious to me but then even Luzon was unknown to some of us down south. The Middle East, America and Europe could have been all the same to me. I had seen foreigners but not often because our island is no longer safe for them. Some tourists were kidnapped from a bus a few years ago. All I knew was that when people went away to work, they became richer and the money helped their families. I also knew that sometimes they didn't come back and that was sad.

'One day I remember some women talking with my mother. I was washing corn under the tap which the houses in our area all shared together. Some of them were cleaning local cabbage and fish for cooking. One woman said that it was wrong to let girls go away from the family to work. My mother said she didn't know but if it would make life easier for the family, perhaps it wouldn't be a bad thing. It all depended on the job, she said, and whether there would be someone to look after the girls.'

She looks down and sighs as she remembers how they had talked on and on.

One of them had spoken about problems girls had sometimes in Manila and they lowered their voices and sent her inside. She can see that day clearly. It is warm and the sun is shining down through the banana leaves into the courtyard. She remembers yellow and green, and the blue of her mother's dress and scarf, the yellow corn and the cloudy water which runs out of the red plastic basin, and the black ants which run away when she spills the water where she has washed the vegetables for the evening meal.

Hana looks out across the courtyard again – now grey and white in the mid-morning sun, while inside, the visitors' room is in shadow and cold, for it is January.

# 2

# May 1998

She seemed to have little choice really. Nevertheless, she is happy. It is exciting to be lining up with other girls her age at the wharf. The ferry has been sitting there for six hours, though it was supposed to have gone two hours ago. That isn't strange, they told her.

Her father sits down by the gate talking with the other men from Cotabato. He isn't happy about her going. He thinks it would be better for her to marry Gammal. They have known each other since she was a child and are related. He is a good boy and she would make him a proper wife.

Hana had wanted more, though. To finish high school might be nice, though no one in her family had done that. If her parents wanted one less to look after and if they hoped for some extra help, why not find work somewhere? That had not been easy in Cotabato. Her mother was reluctant to accompany her to Davao to the agency which had recently been set up but it seemed the only way to satisfy her energetic and anxious daughter.

That was over six months ago. Her application has been successful and has been sent to Manila, where she is now to go for further training before setting off to some place about which she knows nothing. The agency will decide for her. It had not seemed so bad when six others from the same village were selected for work.

A woman from the agency accompanies them and explains the whole procedure to the concerned parents. Their daughters will be chaperoned all the way. They will find good and respectable jobs. Visas will be arranged and they will probably be able to come back to visit after a year or so. In the host country they will have friends from their own country and religious organisations to keep in touch with them.

One of the other young women is her cousin, destined for Singapore, though they do not know that yet. Several of them have put their ages up. They look older, or try to, and are strong enough to do any work. They know they need passports and visas but the agency will take care of these details. All they have to do is learn and be prepared to work hard in an exciting new environment.

She looks at her father again and swallows hard, trying not to cry. She has never been away from home before – at least not so far away. She has told her parents that she will probably go to work in a Muslim family. That seems to reassure them. She promises to write. Several others are Muslim too – all from good families.

'Let's find a bunk before they are all taken. There are others here from different towns but they all have agency stickers on their blouses.' Marita is a Catholic and a few years older than Hana. Like many Filipinas, she has a short name too – Rita. She has a sister who is a nun. The sisters at the local school think Rita would be a likely prospect for the convent but Rita is not ready to tie herself down so quickly.

It seems a good start to have someone wanting to look after her. She follows Rita into the small cabin which is to be home for the next two days while they travel to Manila. As it turns out, there are seven other 'agency girls', as they call themselves, in the cramped room. For most it is an adventure. None of them has ever been to Manila before. Some have heard stories. Others are quite nervous about the whole process but appear cheerful in case people think they are too young to cope with working abroad.

They are given meal packs for lunch and vouchers for the next day's meals. It turns out to be quite an event lining up with other passengers. In each case it is the same – rice, a watery green vegetable and a small piece of boiled fish. The food is not particularly tasty but their hunger, fresh air and the excitement of travelling with other friends their own age makes up for whatever is missing in the cuisine.

Lucy checks all the recruits several times a day. She under-stands the nervousness, curiosity and never-ending questions of the young women. She has seen it all before, though she has never worked overseas herself. She knows clearly the recruitment procedure since she has been through it with several other groups by this stage. It will not be plain sailing for the men and women they place in work abroad but it seems to offer more prospects than staying at home. Reports back vary, though.

'I hope we get to Manila. I know these ferries have a bad name. They sink if they are overloaded so I hope we have no mayors or their wives today.'

They laugh. Living with uncertainly is part of their lives, though it is predictability which both want to escape.

'Where do you think you'll go?' Rita asks as they lean over the rails.

'I hope I go to the Gulf or countries near there because people there will understand me and I've heard that the money is really good. Perhaps I won't have to be away too long if they pay well and my parents might let me study or maybe they will forget about me having to marry Gammal. I really am not interested in him even though my father says I will learn to like him as a husband as time goes on.'

'I don't care where I go – anything to get away for a while too. I'm not ready for a husband yet but I want a chance to get to know some boys as friends as well. My sister decided she could do without them but I often wonder whether she is really sure about it. I've also heard that some priests have left and joined the fighters in the hills. That's a big thing for Catholics, you know. My brother told me that in Cebu, the big sugar men were after one of them a couple of years back. He had helped the people organise for better conditions. You don't have priests and nuns in your religion, do you?'

It seems strange to Hana that young men and women would promise not to marry for their whole lives. Though she is not interested in marriage either right now, celibacy is a strange notion to her. Women are more respected when they do marry in Islam. This seems natural. However, these nuns are honest women, she knows, and they pray and help people, so that is a good thing. It is not such a strange thing that Catholic priests should become involved in politics. Their own religious men teach them things which seem to weave religion and everyday problems together. It is their duty to make things better and to protect their religion and their values.

'Have you ever had a boyfriend?'

'Yes, but not a serious one. He's gone to work overseas too, so I thought why not me? He's working in a hotel in Thailand. It's a good job and he sometimes gets money on the side by driving tourists around in hire cars on his day off, his brother told me. It's OK for us to have boyfriends but not to do anything – you know.'

Hana nods. She knows only to well. Whether they are Catholics or Muslims, Filipino girls are respectable. She knows some of them marry foreigners to get away but they are good wives generally. Sometimes they leave their husbands, she has heard, but this was because of the men. Women who want to marry foreigners are being warned by government departments of all the problems. This is not really her concern, though. She doesn't know of any Muslim women who have married overseas and she is sure she will eventually return to marry in Mindanao.

Again Hana remembers her father standing on the wharf. Her mother hadn't come with them and their farewell had been sad. She promised she would write and that she would come home if she was unhappy or lonely. Deep down, she knows that she cannot do this, though, because she has to help the family and running away from difficulties isn't in her nature.

Once it is dark and there are no more lights from boats or small islands to be seen across the water, the two young women go down to their cabin. The chatting crowd makes them feel light-hearted again and at that stage it is a sense of companionship rather than homesickness that lulls them to sleep.

The next days pass more or less like the first, though the ferry stops at several ports to collect other travellers. This time there are tourists among them, mainly people with backpacks who don't look wealthy, though she knows they must be if they can travel around their islands and to so many different countries. Hana is too shy to talk with these foreigners, though several of the other girls do. This provides a whole new topic of conversation in the cabin that evening.

'They are not married but they travel together. I wonder if they sleep together.'

There is general laughter and Hana feels embarrassed. She realises from the talk which follows that although she knows a lot, she has little experience of sexual urges and certainly no encounters yet. This has to wait. However, in a crowded house it is almost impossible not to know about such things, but it was different with foreigners. They have different customs.

One of their group is still on deck, talking with one of the tourists. 'Maybe she won't make it to Manila with us.'

There is more laughter and perhaps just some twinge of envy that the friendship brewing up on deck might develop into something permanent which would lead to a better life. A delicious feeling of something forbidden about to happen both repulses and intrigues several of the drowsy recruits. More than one of them falls asleep wondering what a Westerner would be like as a lover but as few of them know what any lover is like at this stage, they can only dream.

She wakes with a jolt, aware that there is movement around her. They have berthed.

Manila! This is what she has prepared for, or so she thinks. There is noisy activity in the cabin. The young women have few belongings but had packed them neatly and with pride the evening before. This morning, each of them wears something new. Several have put on lipstick. Hana has a long blouse over her narrow ankle-length skirt, and over her jeans Rita wears a long pink T-shirt with Gucci embroidered in large letters.

Her eyes sparkle as she catches Hana's hand. 'Come on! Lucy is waiting for us near the restaurant.'

There is time for hot milky tea but nothing else as the passengers line up to leave the ferry. As men and women are being met by staff from other recruiting agencies, the band of young women from Mindanao feel reassured to have their own escort. Generally they are younger than many other recruits.

As Hana pushes and manoeuvres her way along the gangway, she holds her bag and small packages tightly. She had thought the Davao wharf was busy but she has never seen anything like this. She does not recognise the writing on some of the big ships, though she has seen Chinese on some of the Mindanao stores. Here ships seem to have arrived from everywhere. It is like a kitchen at home – the heart of the place. Cranes lift huge cargo in wooden crates. Small men bend double under weights too great for them. Little boys run in and out on tasks assigned by deck hands and dock workers.

She dodges a motor scooter carrying mail bags. Her heart begins to beat as she wonders where she is and what she is doing here.

Lucy calls them with a laugh. 'Come on! They're waiting for us.' Lucy laughs and shows them the special jeepney the agency has sent.

After a few minutes on the road, Hana is glad she wears a scarf today. She holds it tight against her nose and mouth. This is what pollution means. The others cough. Rita's eyes water but this time in reaction to the smoke and fumes. Even Lucy seems pale, though she has lived on and off in Manila for years. The roads are wide and there seems to be little pattern to the cars, trucks and jeepneys blasting horns and weaving in and out, barely missing each other. Few of them pay attention to the traffic police unless they draw up alongside and wave them to the side of the road. She begins to have second thoughts about leaving Cotabato.

The welcome from the agency is brisk and businesslike but not unkind.

'She's more like a Madam,' one of the girls giggles.

Hana wonders what she means as she faces the large woman dressed in red and black, wearing large, silver earrings. She speaks loudly and smiles too much, welcoming them, explaining they have passed the initial screening stages and that they will be placed in specific jobs or with agencies within the countries they selected or those which will be selected for them. In the meantime, they will receive some training which will be charged to them with their fee and visa repayment once they start work.

It takes over an hour for the paperwork to be completed for their little group, though Hana is not exactly sure what the documents mean. Lucy explains they are routine – fees for the agency, costs for travel, visa application forms, passport application and other forms with details about next of kin. Hana writes her birth year as 1980, though she is fifteen years old.

After a mid-morning snack of Chinese *siopau* buns and tea, the Mindanao recruits meet others at the office to collect new passports. These women are all headed for the Middle East, many of them to Gulf countries, rich from oil and the business and industry set up from its profit. Hana hopes that she will follow them. *We understand each other*, she thinks.

Already her parents had arranged for her to stay with a family in a Muslim area of Manila, not far from Quiapo district. The others are also to stay in central Manila. Hana's father has friends in the area and knows they live somewhere near the Manila Golden Mosque and Cultural Centre. It should be a good place for his daughter.

Her spirits lift as the jeepney passes the mosque. It is truly beautiful. Imelda Marcos had the mosque built more than thirty years before, a fact which seems strange because Hana has never heard anything good said about the Marcos family. Even Catholics had been heard to criticise them – priests and activist alike. She knew their troubles were the caused by that ex-president, his army and others like them.

Whatever the political reality, the mosque is a real draw-card for southerners. When she visits it the next day, Hana is able to recognise Maranaos, Maguindanaos like herself and some Tausugs. However, she discovers that not all of these people get on well together, in spite of their common culture and religion. The Tausug and Maguindanao people complain that the Maranaos have special privileges because they always have more representatives in any meeting with city officials. This is to reach conflict point when the city officials some time later decide to get rid of the shanty town in the Muslim area and destroy the mainly Maguindanao and Tausug dwellings while allowing the Maranaos to stay longer in their part of the neighbourhood.

The house where she stays is shared with another family but is not as crowded as some others in Quiapo. People speak badly of this district in general, she finds out. Many say it is the gangster area and drugs are sold here. These things Hana does not know at first but her knowledge broadens over the next few weeks.

In all, she stays three months in the Quiapo house, travelling by jeepney twice a week to the Domestic Training Centre. Here she learns the sorts of things which would be relevant in a house more sophisticated than the one in which she has lived in Cotabato. She learns basic things about child care, although many of the lessons she finds boring as she has had plenty of practice looking after younger brothers and sisters when her mother was busy. She learns other things too, such as answering the telephone, using a vacuum cleaner, polishing silver and cooking meals quite different from the simple fare she knows best.

She writes short letters home, nothing memorable and quite like those of the other recruits, reflecting homesickness for her mother and the girls in the family and neighbourhood.

*Dearest Mama*

*I am glad to be here because everyday means one closer to working overseas and I am glad to help you. Perhaps I shall be lucky and be sent to a country with our religion so they will understand me and I shall understand them easily. I miss the quiet of our village but life in this big city is interesting. The training is funny sometimes but I really don't learn anything new. I have some friends and this is really wonderful. You would like them. Don't worry about me.*

*Kiss my father and all the children for me.*
*Your loving daughter Hana*

It is during this time that she meets Alim. He is also a Muslim but different from the boys she has known at home. He has lived in Manila since he was a small child.

His father has a good voice and Hana loves to listen to him singing as he drives the jeepney through the streets around Quiapo – always Tagalog, folk songs and radio pop songs which they all know from hearing them in fancier jeepneys. It was in one of these that Hana had met Alim. They sat next to each other as she travelled to the Centre. He sometimes drove for his father and knew so much about their area that Hana looked out for him whenever she needed to know directions. Eventually she began to wait for him particularly. He was cheerful and was kind to her. He knew her name but did not make it obvious to people that he was giving her a free ride.

The day he asked her to meet him to visit the city sights, her heart gave a little leap and she felt light-headed. For the first time, she really gazed at herself in the mirror. What did he see? She wore no make-up but had large green eyes. Her mother used to tell her that these were her highlights, her assets. She decides that for this special occasion she will leave her hair loose. Only occasionally does she wear a scarf here and that is usually for religious festivals. Generally, like the other women in Quiapo, she dresses in the fashion of most other poor women in Manila, often in jeans and a T-shirt. This day would be no different but she will take extra care so that Alim notices.

Many months later, she looked back on that happy day with Alim. He knew so much but at the same time he made her feel so special, so clever. He was kind and she remembered over and over again how he had looked at her and said that he wished she was not going away. No one had ever spoken to her like that and Hana remembered that when she looked into the mirror again that evening she looked pretty.

Their friendship grew. It was sweet to Hana. In some ways it was

25

like a close friendship she had had with some girls when she was younger. There was plenty of fun in it and they laughed a lot but there was something else there which Hana had never experienced before. She thought about Alim more and more. Sometimes she discovered something she had never seen before or she observed scenes which she knew Alim would have commented on gleefully, sadly or thoughtfully. Along with Rita, he was her best friend at that time and she found herself singing on those days when she knew they would meet.

For these reasons and some other sadness she could not identify, Hana wanted less and less to leave Manila and Quiapo, in spite of the noise, confusion and fumes and in spite of the police who patrolled day and night, making a show of batons and guns as they walked down alleyways and into yards where young men gathered in conversations, often innocent.

It began to dawn on her slowly that even though working overseas would make life easier for her family in Cotabato, she would be separated from her new friend. So it was not strange that when Rita arrived at the house earlier than they had planned one evening, Hana felt like a fish which shrivels up when it is taken from the water, or a baby bird falling too soon from its nest. The people at the agency had said that their permits had come through more quickly this time. Of their group, three were to go to Kuwait. Hana, Rita and the other two had been accepted for another Gulf country, not so far away, though far enough for them not to see each other again. They were to report to the agency's office early next morning.

This was the beginning of a great change in their lives and in Hana's particularly.

# 3

# August 1998

The next three days disappeared and became like details in a dream long past, with only a word or scene here and there creeping back like a dog which has been kicked – lingering, or bringing warmth for kindnesses unnoticed. There were more forms to be completed. Last-minute briefings filled them with that nervous excitement which comes with the new and the unknown. They asked each other many questions they were too shy to ask Lucy or the agency workers. Contact addresses were promised.

Alim and his father had taken Hana to their small home for a final dinner with the family. Considering their simple lifestyle, they had prepared a feast. Hana knew this but could not eat. Alim was very quiet – quieter than she had ever known him. She wondered if he was ill or whether he too was feeling the way she was. As they left her at her house that last evening, he gave her a small package. He had written a verse on the back of a postcard of the Golden Mosque. *Blessings and peace wherever you go, blessings and peace all to you show.* Later she framed it and kept it on her table in another country far from here.

'This will always remind you of Quiapo and of your friends here,' he whispered. As he walked away, he turned and over his shoulder called out, 'And of me.' His raised his fist, clutched in a gesture of strength as the jeepney moved off.

Hana had an ache deep down inside her like that she had had at the Davao wharf as she watched her father. She cried that night before she fell into an uneasy sleep.

The seven Mindanao recruits, and several other men and women they had met at the agency in Manila, stood with them expectantly in the departure terminal. This time Lucy was also going with them to the Gulf to join a recruitment agency. Hana and Rita were to see much of her over the next year.

Lucy's calm contrasted with the nervous excitement of other waiting workers. Some, like Hana, had second thoughts about leaving the Philippines but it was too late to voice nagging doubts. Once they had moved past the immigration desk, they knew there was no turning back, not now and perhaps not for several years.

Novelty offset nervousness in the end. People joked about Philippine Airlines always being late, but this time they were to fly Gulf Air to Karachi, where they would change flights again, so they would never know about their own national carrier. The stub was torn off the departure card and Hana and Rita kept close together. At least they would be sitting next to each other. The smell of fuel turned Hana's stomach as she walked across the tarmac to the plane. She had not been able to eat breakfast that morning. At least it was not too hot, though August was a hot month in Manila.

'I'm glad I still have you as my friend, Rita. I hope they put us together.'

'So am I. This is a real adventure, isn't it?'

Hana glanced at her friend and saw the healthy, shining skin which seemed to glow in anticipation, though she felt as though all life had drained from her, her face without expression now the colour of an old faded photograph.

'I think I'm going to be sick,' she said as the engine roared for take-off and she saw the ground below from her window seat.

Rita called the hostess, who handed Hana a paper bag. She leant over and lost the meal of the previous night.

Perhaps it was a touch of food poisoning or just a fit of nerves as Lucy said, but in any case she felt better after it. It was like leaving all the old and starting out, empty for the new location to fill her with different encounters.

The whole trip was a new experience. Nobody bothered with seat belts in cars in the Philippines, so buckling up in the plane amused them. Seats reclined and were straightened again. Earphones made the women giggle. Hana tuned in to Island Music and pretended that it sounded like music from Mindanao. Although the aeroplane food was not to her taste, she ate the rice greedily because she felt much better now that her stomach was empty. There were toilets to explore and the in-flight movie to watch, although this did not mean much to Hana, whose English was limited. Her English studies at school had been very formal and bookish and she was to discover in this new country that she had less English than she supposed.

When Rita came back from the toilets, she reeked of cheap eau de cologne. Hana sneezed, told her how nice she smelt, promptly went down and dowsed herself in it, and sneezed again.

A voice over the intercom told passengers that they would soon be landing at Quaid-e-Azam International Airport, Karachi. Hana missed the other details but it didn't matter, as Lucy had sent the message along the line that they were to hold tight to tickets and passport, to bring their cabin luggage and stay close to her. Hana wondered how other Filipinas like her managed if they had no one to show them the way.

She looked from the window as the plane landed with a light bounce. Flags – green with white crescents – fluttered in the breeze. Green PIA trucks sped across the tarmac to the Gulf-bound plane while green and yellow minibuses buzzed around like honey birds searching for nectar. Several security men with guns and mobile phones wandered nonchalantly around the parked vehicles. Hana was disappointed as there was nothing unusual about the terminal. The building surrounded by flat wasteland was imposing but in size alone.

As the passengers were finally ushered into a large waiting room with their transit cards, she marvelled at how many women wore scarves and veils here. Certainly Muslims in Manila were fairly easy about these things but, even for Hana, this was the first of many things from a vastly different life to confront her in what would turn out to be a completely foreign culture.

One could say that international airports are more or less the same anywhere and that only the mixture of people differs. For the transiting Filipinas and travelling workers from Pakistan, many of them Pukhtuns from the north-west frontier, this was a new episode in their lives. Few had seen an airport before this trip. Many were leaving wives and children behind.

The Filipinas were also surprised to see little boys lining up in the departure lounge. They looked no more than five or six years old. Later they learnt that the children were trained as camel jockeys; the fortunate ones among them ended up in households where Filipina or Sri Lankan maids became substitute mothers to them. More often, though, these children passed through childhood without the company of women, and usually without the nurturing little children crave. As yet, all of these things were mysteries to the new recruits.

This mass movement of workers to the Gulf was an exodus but these people were not looking for the Promised Land. Theirs was a dream of wealth – vain in many cases – the golden calf which would make life better for their generation. Just as sailing ships in centuries past carried settlers to strange lands to establish new ways of living and in turn, to build their own nations, so this plane taking workers to the Gulf replaced the great immigrant vessels of old. To some eyes this looked less like a departure terminal and more like a refugee post.

Today this was a different departure terminal, though. Among the waiting passengers were many travellers – poor and unkempt. Their dress was rough and they gazed at the far-eastern female travellers, in jeans and T-shirts too revealing to men from conservative, rural communities. The north-west frontier people who made up the bulk of the Pakistani contingent looked out of place here. They were awkward. Chappals were rough. Turbans denoted their region. *Shalwah kameez,* more frequently than not, were dirty with rough, dark material, distinguishing northerners and border people from the lowlanders and southerners in their pale, pastel colours. There was a wildness about the northerners but also an aura of honour and dignity to match that of the *bedu* they would encounter on the Arabian peninsula.

The thing that struck all the Filipinas on this flight, though, was that the Pakistani contingent was totally male while their own group was predominantly female. Not only the numbers but the size of these men outweighed them. These were big men towering over the small people of south-east Asia – tribal people, proud in their bearing, rulers of their lands, now cowering to join queues of workers with whom they had little in common and men who had been their traditional rivals, feuding for generations. Many more of them would come directly on flights from Peshawar in the rugged north-west, workers now, so important in the grinding labour, constructing small desert skeikhdoms.

Hana suddenly felt overcome. She had come from a Muslim community where poverty and a common struggle over the years in Mindanao produced a sense of oneness, a community of men and women. In her family, if few of the girls had education beyond primary school, neither did the boys. Curfew rules were more a matter of common sense than regulations imposed to control women and reduce them to property.

Then, along with the others, who were feeling hesitant and nervous about the new venture on which they were embarking, Hana forgot her own misgivings as she watched the little boys fidgeting tiredly. They seemed oblivious to what lay before them. Why, she wondered, were they sending these children away? This would be unheard of in the Philippines, she thought, without knowing the plight of some children in her own country in the hands of some tourists.

Their stopover was an hour and a half but because Hana had not slept well the night before it seemed much longer. While she had found the Ninoy Aquino Airport in Manila busy, the one in Karachi gave her a headache.

She was finally beginning to doze when she heard a voice in a language she could not decipher calling over the intercom.

'Time to go again.' Lucy had rounded a few of them up and had moved to the front of the line.

The usher told them not to worry about being separated because their new boarding cards had seat numbers written on them. This time,

Rita and Hana were both quiet, surrounded by men who seemed more curious than anything else, but they felt intimidated.

Gulf Air was again to carry them on the last section. Hana admired the blue and beige uniforms of the attendants. They were smart, with a veil which enticed more than anything else. How strange it was, she thought, that the hostesses looked European.

This time, the journey felt more like a bus ride through Manila. Everyone had a seat but somehow the plane seemed crowded. Perhaps it was because the men walked up and down the aisles looking at the passengers as they did so. Hana wanted to go to the toilets at the back of the plane now but she was too shy to walk down and wait with the queue of men which never seemed to diminish. There was no movie this time and it seemed that no sooner had they received a meal than the hostess was collecting the trays again. Hana refused the drinks because they would only make her uncomfortable situation more desperate.

Setting down in Dhahabi was a relief for all of the Manila crowd and, with a long flight and very early morning, the novelty was beginning to wear thin now.

There was not much to see of the airport. Things were quiet for the early morning arrival. As Hana and her friends had little luggage, the customs officers did not trouble them much. Passport control had been a different matter, however, with a string of questions which Lucy had stood by to answer and interpret. Hana thought there was a lot of paperwork. Everything about this job seemed to involve paperwork. There was also much talk about sponsors. In their case, the agency had arranged the legal aspects well. It also had a branch in Dhahabi with three prominent nationals or local citizens leading the management. This made their movement through the immigration formalities swift, and once more Hana was grateful for Lucy's presence.

Two yellow-uniformed Filipinas, employees of a local travel agency, were waiting for them in the arrivals' section.

One of them knew Lucy and greeted her warmly. 'I hope you're not going to regret this,' she said in Tagalog.

Lucy laughed. 'I've been waiting for this. It should be good. I know lots of people here and someone at the embassy too.'

There was no money to change at the bank. An allowance in *dirhams* which they would repay from their first salary was to be given to them later that day.

Once again the recruits were bundled into a hired minibus and taken to a hotel in what turned out to be a fairly rough part of the town. This didn't matter in the long run as the women had already been placed in work, so it was only a matter of finalising permits, which the agency handled well. Four women shared a room. The evening was strangely cool so it did not bother them but for the groups sharing in the hot months, such accommodation was oppressive. The room was noisy as other occupants shared the bathroom at the end of a passage next to their room but they slept quickly after a day which had been too long.

If the farewells in Davao and Manila had been sad, this wrench seemed the ultimate. Now they were on their own.

'We must try to see each other on our days off.'

'Yes, and we must get to know this city so that we can find places to meet. Perhaps we will be able to telephone each other. At least for you it is easier. You understand their customs, Hana.'

'But it's different from Cotabato.'

None of the women had seen the desert yet. The contrast between the flat, grey sands with the colourless sky which blanketed the city that afternoon, and the lushness of Mindanao's forest was stark. What they could see was more like something from the science fiction movies they had received on local neighbourhood video screens. Tall, slim, white skeletons like wedding cakes grew out of a barren, lifeless landscape. Hana thought of ugly eruptions on smooth, unblemished skins sent to torment self-conscious young men and blossoming women. One couldn't tell where they would erupt next and, as the months passed, high-rise buildings like this would grow as they watched.

Because the agency's local branch had already arranged for the placement of many of the new recruits, Hana, Rita and their friends had barely two days to acclimatise themselves to this port city. They were taken on a half day's sightseeing tour which mainly involved visits to the shopping complexes popping up along the city's Corniche and Creek areas. Concrete lollypop boxes from a distance; inside, masses of shops, glittering with chandeliers, gold-plated signs and fashion, household decorations and electrical goods from every country imaginable, all to excite the new recruits. They visited the fish and vegetable markets near the port and large supermarkets whose names were to become commonplace for them, religious incantations they heard repeated over and over in voices tinged with reverence and awe.

'You won't need to worry about how to get here,' another Filipina from the agency said. 'Usually drivers from the houses where you work will bring you. If you can drive, some of you may be asked to drive the women to local markets. Here they call them *souqs*. It will be good for you if you can learn some Arabic. In many houses, people can't speak much English.' She watched them and went on, 'And often the women can't speak English at all.'

'Well, how are we going to manage?' Rita gasped softly.

'Don't worry. Everyone gets by. Use the international language – signs. But believe me, you will learn a few phrases of Arabic very soon. Tomorrow we'll teach you some basic terms and you can spend the rest of the day practising with each other. At least in our agency we try to put you in a house where someone speaks your language. The other workers will teach you anyway.'

A short while later, with the new workers seated on anything which had the appearance of being solid in the tiny office, an agency woman briefed them with tips useful to keep stored for the right moment. 'Remember, we are a respectable agency and we have found you sponsorship already. If you decide to leave your work, you will have to face the problem of new sponsorship. Don't be fooled by empty promises. Be careful, because not everyone here knows our Filipino culture. Sometimes they think the wrong things of us because we are friendly and outgoing.' She looked around and guessed that at least some of the young women, including Hana, did not understand.

'Some, though not many of us, have got themselves into work which we don't encourage.' She paused again. 'This is a male society and this is stronger than any religion. It's the same in the Philippines. *Machismo*, remember? OK, so we've done our job. You've been placed in a job. You have sponsorship and you are obliged to repay fees which we have paid for you over the past months. You have a smoother start than some. Be sensible. I know you are good workers. Everyone knows that.'

They were told to register their names with the embassy by filling in one more form. At least Hana felt her understanding of bureaucracy was improving, even if her English wasn't. Alim had helped her a little with that. He was used to meeting foreigners in his job and for young people in Manila the trend was to speak English with an American accent, even though America was not regarded well because of its military base not far from the capital. Some were quite good at it, with 'Hey, Joe' and other slang phrases interspersed. Rita had helped her too. She had learnt English from the nuns at school. Some of them belonged to American and Irish religious congregations and had been made to speak English in their novitiate years and continued to communicate daily in their convents where there were still older nuns from European countries. Many of these had learnt Tagalog and liked to use it, but English was seen as the way ahead, a sign of development in their vibrant, struggling country.

It was all too new for Hana to take much in. She could not identify this with what she knew, though a Luzon woman who had spent years working in Manila told her that the high buildings and office blocks in this Gulf commercial centre reminded her of Quezon City, metro Manila's diplomatic area.

For Hana, these constructions bore no resemblance to the shanty areas around Quiapo, shanty towns which the Manila Council was to raze, claiming they were ridding the city of health hazards and drug dens. Hana and others knew when that happened that this was part of a campaign which extended right up from Mindanao – apprehension of the military of rebel factions which included their own community.

'We'll have to be good at bargaining if we are to see each other,' Rita complained when she discovered that there was little public transport – nothing like the jeepneys in their own towns and cities. 'It seems too far to walk from different centres in this city and they say it stays really hot for up to ten months of the year. We should be used to that but it's like an oven outside.'

'I'm scared of the traffic,' Hana responded. 'It's bad in Manila but this is different. I don't think cars will let you get across.' Already she had had the experience of cars playing with her attempts to cross the divided highway outside the Bur Jaman shopping mall.

There was also no doubt as they looked in the stores that they would not be doing much buying. For some of them, this was an adventure away from home. For all of them, this was the way to get ahead, to help their families. In most cases it was a way out of the poverty which haunted many Filipinas. In *peso* terms, their promised salaries meant a lot of money. Six hundred *dirhams*, the salary which Hana had heard she was likely to receive from housekeeping each month, converted to more than four thousand *pesos*. This was more than an ordinary worker could earn in the Philippines in many, many months. They were all determined to save. In any case, the prices in luxury shopping centres still belonged to another world, a world they seemed to be unable to enter easily.

The fresh recruits signed the last form, and the agency woman looked at the Mindanao group with a fleeting touch of sadness, or was it also apprehension? 'Take care of yourselves.'

# 4

# September 1998

It came as a surprise when Hana learnt of her employment the next day. She thought she would care for someone's children or at least do housework with a family.

'It will only be temporary because they are in urgent need for someone to help with cleaning. I'm sure you'll do well and as soon as we get someone else, we'll find you another position,' the manager of the agency had said.

She was to work as a cleaner at Sandoz Beauty Salon in Al Shams, about one hour's drive from the city. She had never been to a hairdresser herself. Her mother cut her hair when it was necessary. Later, her own friends did it. She wore it rather long anyway. Hana wanted to protest but she knew there was little point. It was a job and she did have sponsorship and maybe it would not be too bad. She would be working with women in any case. Another woman from their group was also going to Al Shams. She was to work as a cleaner too but at the Intercontinental Hotel.

At least in the beauty salon, she would be saved the crowds she would have to meet working at a hotel. She could not be comfortable with the idea of being in such a place. From Manila stories, she knew that alcohol was available and illicit affairs were carried on in hotels, all of which packaged together confronted the gentle but definite code of her family and her own Maguindanao community.

A bigger disappointment was that Rita was to stay in the city, which meant their earlier plans of meeting regularly would be curtailed. This seemed to have been the pattern since leaving Cotabato, and each separation left Hana feeling as though she was slowly coming out of a long illness.

Another minibus picked them up from their hotel. There were already some other newly arrived workers seated in the back – two Sri Lankan women, a Bangladeshi and two Pakistanis. Hana recognised them from their clothes. The three men spoke together in Urdu, or that is what one of the other women called it. Some were going to the hotel. A new wing had been opened there and new workers were being recruited from outside the country. Others were moving from different hotel chains or were between sponsors, making them vulnerable and liable to be changed. The Sri Lankans thought this was a good placement.

They were all astounded to reach the desert on the Dhahabi–Al Shams road. This time it was real desert. There were sand dunes as far as they could see in some places. Sands were red, then golden and, though most of them had come from green and tropical countries, they also thought that in its own way this desert was beautiful in the late afternoon sun.

The biggest excitement were the camels. The Pakistanis, one a Pukhtun from the north-west frontier and the other a Baluchi from the border further south, knew camels and thought it strange that these other men and women were so excited whenever one was sighted.

These creatures were strange and beautiful – animals giving pride to the Arabs who knew them more now for their racing prowess and less as pack or vehicular animals who could find their way through these deserts of nothingness and sameness.

The people who worked in hotels and who met foreigners were also to find out that, like them, others too had almost romantic feelings for the camels, used more these days for safari tours into the Empty Quarter.

The young women did not know what these Frontier men knew, that little boys came here to be trained as jockeys. Some would say they were too young to be working but eventually they would earn a great deal of money once it was converted to be sent back home.

There were some small settlements along the highway – an agricultural research station and a rest house at one place, a petrol station at another, and camel farms dotted through the sand dunes much of the way.

Being able to see so far across the sands could only be compared with looking out to sea for Hana. One never knew what was on the other side or if it could be reached safely but, as with Filipino men of the sea familiar with the moods of the waters, so desert *bedu* gazed like new lovers across these sands. Maybe they also used stars to guide them, she mused. She liked the red and yellow sands. They lifted her spirits in a way that the grey sands of Dhahabi could not.

By the time they reached Al Shams, a pretty town with tree-lined streets which might almost be boulevards, the evening prayer call boomed out through loud speakers on little mosques. Hana pulled her scarf over her head, the scarf she had adopted for Dhahabi streets where she saw more women covered than she had expected.

The bus dropped her at the beauty salon. Someone would be waiting there for her, they had told her. The driver kept the engine running but did not move, waiting to be sure that she was met.

Sandoz was not a large salon but the sign was imposing. The windows were covered in adhesive film which prevented people seeing in. A sign on the door said 'Ladies Only'. She knocked and turned the handle. It was locked.

'It's prayer time,' the driver called out. 'Try the back door.'

Later she learnt that in some places, shops closed during the evening prayer sessions, unlike Mindanao. This was one of them but the back door was still open and another Filipina met her.

'Mabuhay!' The traditional Filipino welcome warmed her.

Hana talked freely in Tagalog but still spoke haltingly in English because her teachers in Mindanao had been proud of the language which had been adopted for the nation. She had its regional dialect as well and knew a little formal Arabic from her Quranic studies.

The young woman welcomed her in, collected her small bag from the minibus and waved the driver away cheerily. They walked up two steps from the dark entrance into a narrow passageway which led to a small, bright room lined with shelves along three walls holding piles of towels and bottles of shampoo and cosmetics. There was a strange, pungent smell which Hana learned was from chemicals used for perming hair. Another door opened into a welcoming light area which she presumed was the beauty salon. Large mirrors lined both side walls. In front of them, narrow tables with marble surfaces and brass fittings were reflected in the mirrors. Comfortable chairs pushed beneath them matched other furniture scattered around the room. She recognised the rattan; there was plenty of it in the Philippines. Large pots holding artificial plants stood around the room, highlighting low tables piled with glossy fashion magazines. Glass jars holding combs and brushes with brass handles twinkled in the light as small chandeliers overhead moved when the door opened.

'I've been preparing your room and tidying the salon for tomorrow,' the other girl said. 'Because it's Friday, we don't open here. Some places do, but our owners are quite reasonable. As long as everything is ready, they don't mind if I go out for the day.'

For Hana, Friday was the religious day for Muslims but in Mindanao, like all islands in the mainly Catholic Philippines, Sunday was the rest day.

'Let's eat. I had a bigger meal earlier today, so I hope what I've prepared is enough. Put your bag in here first.'

She looked into a tiny room with a small couch beside the door.

'It opens into a bed but they think this is tidier if the other women who work here come up during the day. We can share the cupboard in the corridor for our clothes. I keep my small things in a cupboard like this.' The other young woman, called Nancy, indicated to a low chest of drawers where a vase of artificial flowers sat covering a small lace mat.

To Hana this seemed like a castle – her own room – after years of sharing with brothers and sisters, friends in Quiapo and other recruits on the ferry and the hotel room in Dhahabi.

The two women chatted contentedly while they ate instant noodles and drank Pepsi. Hana's family never had such luxury and in any case her mother said that she had been told in the health classes at the local clinic that this soft drink full of sugar was really unhealthy. For the first time, Hana enjoyed this sense of indulging in the forbidden.

'Our salary isn't bad and we have rooms here and the Pepsi is in the refrigerator whenever we want. It's a pity you are only staying a few months. Our other girl will be back from the Philippines by then. That's why they want you – to do the cleaning because now I have to do all the hairdressing. There's an Indian girl who comes in each day to do the facials. Perhaps we can teach you a few things. They might come in handy.'

They talked for a while longer until Hana sensed her new workmate was slightly agitated and wanted to move. She was tired anyway and had to be up early next morning so was glad to go to the comfort of her own room. She struggled with the foldaway bed which doubled as a settee. It was a surprise to find that Nancy had already put sheets and a light rug on the bed. It folded away so neatly that it was difficult to tell what was there. She wondered why Nancy had looked strangely at her when she had said that this was a handy arrangement when the need arose.

She had another question in her mind some hours later when she woke with a jolt. At first she couldn't remember where she was. There had been so many changes over the last few weeks. Then she knew that she heard it again. Voices were coming from the next room. One belonged to a man. Hana thought this strange because it was late now. She heard Nancy giggle a few times and then the voices quietened down. She started to doze off again and then sat bolt upright as she heard a voice which could only have been Nancy's gasping out and then a scream or squeal or a combination of both, she could no longer tell. At almost the same time, a man groaned and then called out but Hana could not understand what he shouted – then silence.

She did not recognise what she had heard. She waited and wondered if she should go to see what was happening. There was something about these voices that reminded Hana of things she had heard in her childhood, years ago when she lived in the flimsy wooden house above the sea. There was something secret and mysterious about these voices. It wasn't pain or anger or fear that she had heard, so she waited.

It took no time for a door to open nearby. Perhaps it was Nancy's room. There were no more voices. She heard footsteps pass her room and go downstairs. Someone followed. The back door opened and closed and she heard the bolt being pulled across. A car started, slowly pulled away and then roared down the street. A door nearby closed again and there was silence.

Hana heard these sounds many times over the two months she was living at the salon but she never questioned Nancy, who was always less communicative the following day. Hana found this friendship quite different from the one she had with Rita. With her everything was shared so closely, and this new silence made her homesick for close friends.

The following morning a whole new world began to unfold before her. Again the early prayer call from a nearby mosque woke her. Nancy called her soon afterwards saying she had breakfast ready.

She showered in the small *hammam* sometimes used by customers. It was a real pleasure to have hot water on tap like this. There was little natural light in the salon except for their kitchen upstairs. This was an exclusive area for women so outsiders should not be able to see in. The first rays of the morning sun crept into the kitchen while the two young women ate their simple breakfast.

The salon manageress, a Lebanese woman called Najla, arrived at seven-thirty. By then Nancy and Hana had already started, wiping bench-tops and placing towels beside washbasins ready for use. On other days there were shampoo bottles to refill, boxes to unpack from distribution companies, and combs and brushes to disinfect before the doors opened for customers at eight o'clock.

Najla wore a long burgundy-coloured coat and a white scarf which covered her hair. She was beautiful and much taller than the two Filipinas. Like Hana, she was very pale, an attribute which many of the customers tried to emulate. Whitening agents were often used on the faces of Arab and Indian women who came for cosmetic treatment. Hana had never thought much about her fair skin before, although people often remarked on it. Probably it was because she spent so much time indoors, even at home in Mindanao. In her family, skin colour did not matter, though she knew with wealthy Filipinas it was an added sign of beauty, promoted by Western magazines and films.

After a brief and sincere welcome, Najla outlined Hana's duties. 'Because you have never worked in a beauty salon before, you need to concentrate on sweeping up hair after it is cut. We have to dispose of this carefully and I'll show you how later. It is important to have everything clean here because we have many customers from the university and foreign companies, as well as young ladies from important families. They also like this salon to be modern, so we don't keep the old magazines down here. It will be your job to go to the Intercontinental Hotel each week to see if our subscriptions have arrived.'

Hana wondered if she would see the other recruits who had travelled with her the day before.

'Sometimes you will have to make tea or coffee for our customers. Always use the cups on the top shelf. These are for guests in the salon. Don't chip them when you are washing them.' She outlined other minor duties and added with a smile that they would teach her waxing, as they always needed extra hands for this.

Hana had never seen or heard of waxing and was quite startled when she saw it being done the next day. The customer was a foreign woman with fair hair. Her heavily accented English was smattered with Russian. She had been on holidays in Dhahabi and had come to the Intercontinental Hotel in Al Shams in answer to an advertisement in the employment section of the local English language newspaper. Nancy said she had a local boyfriend from a prominent family who objected to the relationship.

She was taken upstairs to a special couch where she lifted her skirt for the operation. The hot wax smelt – just one more smell among many in the salon. Hana flinched at the ripping sound as the adhesive pulled the hairs from the leg. She wanted to laugh. This seemed such a strange thing to do. Her own smooth legs had never known shaving or waxing. When bikini lines were waxed, she was horrified and was glad she was not going to be involved in this type of work for long.

She heard lots of gossip in the salon, or at least she heard it in translation because Nancy spoke English well and chatted away to the Western women who came in for all types of attention. There were also a few Asian women but prices were generally too high for them. On the whole, the Arab women were young. They came to have their hair coloured and occasionally cut in modern styles, though women from conservative families still wore their hair long.

Many women came to have their nails done. Hana would spend the morning preparing bowls of hot water where customers would soak their hands or feet before having manicures and pedicures.

She also watched from afar as others had relaxing massages on the couch in the upstairs salon. It was a smaller room and was mainly reserved for women having facials – a word covering a lengthy activity which involved applying and removing various creams and lotions. At least this room smelt pleasant as perfumes wafted about in an area not yet affected by the whirling and spinning of fans and grinding air conditioners.

Najla surveyed the work of the three women but did none of it herself. Her position was purely managerial. She stood behind a counter near the front door and collected money as customers left, generally happy with the service they had received at Sandoz Salon. From here she could talk with the Arab women who were waiting to be served. She controlled the phone, speaking in English and Arabic.

Twice while Hana was at the salon, the owner came to visit. This was unusual, she learnt, as most owners checked the progress of their businesses from the bank balance each month.

Najla seemed an efficient manager to Hana, though she had had little experience in business. Nancy confirmed this when she told her that Najla had been to university in Lebanon. She had studied business administration and had accepted the job three years ago when she joined her husband, a lecturer in engineering at the national university nearby. Because her husband had a good job with a high salary, he had been allowed to sponsor his family. Unlike many men in the Gulf, he could bring his wife to join him. They had been married six months at the time but three years later still did not have any children.

'It's his fault,' Nancy had said, 'but he blames her. She is his second wife and the first wife didn't have any children either. One day before you came, I found Najla crying very hard and she must have felt really bad because she told me her husband was saying that he wanted to take another wife. Since then, she hasn't been so friendly to me. Maybe she is embarrassed that she told me.'

Hana understood. She knew how important it was for men to father children. Sometimes in the Philippines, girls who were not married had babies and, even though the families were not happy with them, the boys or men responsible would tell people about it. They were proud to be so strong. Her brother had told her these things when they were both young, though now he would never mention such things to his sister.

Sharing such confidences led Hana to ask Nancy more about sex.

At first, Nancy had been abrupt and not keen to talk but the same evening, as the two of them again sat eating instant noodles, she was more forthcoming. 'Have you ever had a boyfriend?'

Hana told her about Alim and what a good friend he had been.

The other woman listened in silence for some time and then asked if there was anything more.

'What do you mean?'

'Did you ever kiss or make love?' she asked, using a Tagalog phrase which was rougher than Hana had expected her to use.

'Of course not. It's not allowed.'

'But that doesn't mean you don't do it. We all feel like that at first but we get over it.'

She was not clear whether it was the shock or bewilderment at what Nancy seemed to be saying which led her to ask, 'What are you saying, Nancy? Do you do these things?'

Nancy told her that she had a friend, a kind friend who came to see her. He helped her when she was in trouble.

Hana was not sure what she meant but sensed financial benefits were involved. 'Does he come to see you here?'

Nancy seemed to panic. 'Don't say anything. We are not allowed to have men here. You know that because I heard Najla tell you the first day. I have to let him come here now because he will get angry if I don't let him.'

Hana was intensely curious by this time and could not help the probing questions which seemed to pour out. As Nancy answered softly, Hana was aware that she was curiously agitated by the answers. She was breathing heavily.

The boyfriend was married. This was a serious thing in this country. Hana was not to say anything. She was worried that she might become pregnant.

Hana was really shocked now. She knew exactly what that meant. She found it hard to believe Nancy had such a relationship.

'He says that if I don't let him come, he will tell his friends and also tell them that other men have been with me and then I will be deported. There was someone else before but I have stopped that now. I like this man. I would like to get married but there is absolutely no way, not yet anyway.'

By the end of the long conversation, which lasted several hours, Hana's head was spinning. She did not know what to believe. Certainly her workmate appeared in a different light and the next time she heard the two voices in the next room, she felt she could picture what was happening. It disturbed her greatly and she tossed and turned for hours before she finally fell asleep.

From this time on, Hana began to look forward to moving on to her next job. She felt uncomfortable with the sexual affair which was happening within earshot and now felt an accomplice to the activities because she knew what was happening. She also knew there was no way she could become a friend of Najla because the woman held her distance from the others working under her. The Indian beautician was a beauty in her own way but seemed so sophisticated that Hana felt more and more like a village girl. She resented her confined life in Cotabato and was annoyed that she was still like a child in all these things.

There was little to break the day-in day-out pattern of work. Though she had every Friday free, she did not have enough money to go to Dhahabi. Like Rita and the others who had come with her, she had financial repayments for visas, sponsorship and job placement with the agency.

She had four letters in the months she was at Sandoz – two from Alim, both postcards from Manila, a letter from her mother and a card from Rita. Her friend talked a little about her work and the people she had met but did not give any real indication of how she was finding life in Dhahabi. She had been to one Filipino social gathering but met many more of their country people at the Catholic church she attended each Sunday. The priests there were Italian and one had even learnt Tagalog so that he could celebrate Mass in their language once a month. Hana was impressed that a religious person would take this trouble. Rita had told her that many years ago, Catholics celebrated their religious gatherings in Latin just as Muslims the world over pray in Arabic. That had all changed now and local languages were used.

After hearing from Rita, Hana felt homesickness such as she had never experienced before.

The other thing which made the time in Al Shams more difficult was the month of Ramadan. This year it started in late January and went on through February. It meant that there were fewer customers to the salon and the reduced hours of eating seemed to make the working day much longer. Nancy went upstairs for tea and snacks during the day but did not eat in front of Hana and Najla. Najla was more ill-tempered than usual and Hana wondered why, during this fasting month, some people became more nervous instead of more understanding and tolerant.

She had expected to feel more at home in this society than she did. She remembered how she had anticipated feeling one with these people. After all, they shared a common heritage and even some of the *madrassahs* in Mindanao had been funded from Middle Eastern countries.

With Ramadan came a new, unexpected comfort. It was a real delight for Hana to be invited several times to share *iftar* meals with a neighbouring Pakistani family. A relative of theirs had arrived on the same flight as Hana and by coincidence they had come to Al Shams together by minibus.

Each evening, the women prepared the final touches of the meal while the men prayed. Hana was happy helping them. This reminded her of home, though the language was different and the cooking smells were unfamiliar. Each time she visited them, they prepared a special *kebab* which was a speciality of the north west frontier. They also drank *qawa,* sweet green tea flavoured with cardamom. On one visit the men remarked that Hana was too thin and needed fattening up, so the women made another type of tea called *dud pati.* Milk was boiled first and tea leaves and sugar added later. 'You will want to sleep after this,' they had told her.

On one visit, Hana played with the children, who waited expectantly for the older ones who had been fasting.

'That little boy doesn't fast, though. He's too young. He's only seven. He is a jockey anyway and he needs to be strong but not too heavy. He is related to my husband so we bring him with us sometimes if we can.'

The woman explained how the boy lived with the other men who cared for the camels at the farms out of town. The yards where racing camels were penned were in the desert. At this cool time of the year when there were plenty of fresh green herbs sprouting in the small sand dunes, camels roamed wild seeking them out but their search was easy now.

Again Hana wondered about the boy's mother and whether he missed her. She wondered if he went to school. She was interested to know that he knew how to speak Arabic and wished she could learn as easily. Her problem was that too many people around her spoke English. She asked many questions about these small jockeys and wondered how, if the legal age for jockeys in this country was ten, a little boy like this could be riding.

One of the men, by this time finished with his praying, shrugged. 'The boy is doing better than he would be at home. It's the same for all of us. Our money is helping other people in the family a lot. He knows he is doing some good, so he puts up with the difficulty.'

Certainly now, playing with the other children, there were no visible signs of the hardship that the child lived through on the camel farms.

These few occasions with the Pakistani family gave her great happiness. She had missed this atmosphere in the salon environment. Everything there seemed artificial and Nancy was generally too preoccupied to spend evenings walking or chatting with her.

Hana looked forward to the time when she would be living with a real family again.

# 5

# February 1999

Eid had come and gone. If the first weeks of Ramadan had been quiet at the salon, the days before the festival which marked the end of the fasting month were full of movement, noise, new people and an air of celebration. Nancy had said Ramadan was rather like Lent, the month of penance when many Christians performed some good acts or 'went without', mortification she said, in atonement for their sins. Atonement of sins was not how Hana saw the holy month and she doubted whether the local people did either because there seemed to be more eating and celebrating in the evening hours than at any other time of the year. It was as though refraining from food and drink in the daylight hours meant anything else could be done in the hours of darkness. What she could not fail to notice, though, was that customers flocked to the salon in the last week before Eid.

Women of all ages came to Sandoz, where before they had only had their regular customers. Hair was to be coloured, shaped, curled, shortened and hennaed. Hands were to be decorated in the traditional style. Where customarily women had painted henna on each other's hands, beauty salons in the small Gulf country were beginning to take over their role. Hana and Nancy had no practice nor experience in this intricate and lengthy artwork, though the Indian woman who worked at Sandoz was used to it. Najla was happy to bring in several women from other Arab countries to do the henna painting which so many women wanted for Eid, and the cheeriness of these new sessional workers affected the two Filipinas as well.

There were five women in all. They had been coming to do henna painting at the salon for the past three years. They were from Iraq, Jordan and one from Algeria. Hana was mesmerised by their work and when she could escape from the cleaning which never seemed to end at that time, she would hover around and watch their art. Henna was prepared to the right consistency. Smooth bare hands and arms were held open, facing upwards in expectation of the dye which had been used to decorate women's limbs for thousands of years. These days, some young women preferred ready-made templates for the modern patterns but women generally looked with disdain on this method even though the results were highly decorative. Sandoz Salon would accommodate them, however, just as they would offer them the enjoyment of the older, slower and perhaps more relaxing decoration by hand.

Perhaps it was the personal attention of having another woman decide a pattern which suited a particular hand and personality but when Hana was offered the traditional method, she found the experience calming. She felt she was floating as the Algerian woman quietly applied a pattern which her own mother had used.

Pakistani friends invited her to their house for their own henna painting. The women there spent the evening laughing and talking and drinking tea, while the women at the salon continued to refrain from drink in the daylight hours but enjoyed their own Arabic coffee during the late night sessions which the salon now arranged. Nancy had warned her that near Eid, they would stay open all night. Hana's friends could not afford salon prices and were unused to having strangers decorate their hands and feet in any case. These were happier hours for Hana, as she could relax without having to be on the move, cleaning up after customers and their artists.

Sometimes she would lie in bed in those dark minutes before putting her feet to the cold floor in the mornings, thinking back over the previous evening. Often these moments were delicious and she would roll up in a ball or stretch out endeavouring to wake up fully, thinking of her friends and their easy-going warmth with her. If she heard the loud voices of women who had been in the salon repeating in her brain, she would toss and turn until she finally had to get out of bed to escape the chatter and recollections. She had this uneasy feeling if the first thoughts which woke her in the morning were of what had gone on in the room beside her the night before, for Nancy's friends were still visiting her, though less now that the salon had become so busy at night.

Eid had brought special pleasures with it. The two Filipinas were invited to join the Pakistani family and their friends for a picnic to celebrate. Hana had joined them the previous night as well, to find the new moon announcing the end of Ramadan. So many people had been out at the edge of town, looking over the desert where the black sky made moon and stars more pronounced. This reminded her of her childhood, where it was the excitement of being the first one to sight the moon on the eve of Eid and giving the call to other friends, enticing people from their homes.

Taxis collected them from the salon for this day. Everything was given over to the celebration, including the taxis driven by two Frontier men. They climbed into the already packed car with their modest offerings for the meal, hardly necessary once the other women unpacked their boxes of food. There were children with them that day and the little jockey had come again too.

'He's limping. What's wrong?'

'Sometimes they fall from the camels but he's not badly hurt. It happened in a race just before Ramadan started. The men at the camel farm massaged him and the owner asked one of our doctors to look at him. He said it won't take long to get better but he has had too many falls. These days they tie them on with material which sticks together.' She did not know the commercial name of Velcro. 'But one day they were practising and didn't care about it.'

The other children had played ball and Nancy called to Hana to join them but instead she went with the little camel rider, who was pushing a bottle top across the ground with a stick. Neither knew each other's language but were happy together taking turns with the toy.

Everything about that day made Hana smile. The men were friendly and joked like brothers with them. This was different from what she had experienced with other men from the subcontinent who were working in Al Shams. Often when she was shopping or visiting the Intercontinental Hotel to collect the salon's magazines, she sensed men's hungry eyes on her. Sometimes words were uttered or one of them would approach her in the street and ask for something. She was never sure what was said but began to sense that the requests were for sex. She would blush with shame, wanting to scream and cry with indignity at the same time but this was a man's town and she knew that either action would bring the suspecting public gaze upon her.

Once she mentioned it to her Indian colleague at the salon, who had looked at her with some sympathy and had whispered, 'I'm sorry, Hana, but it's because you are Filipina and men here like your women.'

'But I am a Muslim and they should respect us!'

'Respect has nothing to do with it here. We are all the same in their eyes. If we are working, we want money and our families can't look after us or control us any more, so they think.'

For the first time, Hana realised that what the women had talked about with her mother in their village was this. Women without men to care for them, to order and direct them, were women open to any suggestion, especially when it came to money. Resentment began to build up in her.

The Eid picnic day was a family day, though, where the men and women were kind and the children responded with an affection that came with their own sense of being the centre of attention. Nancy had also been affected by the spirit of celebration, though had many questions about one of the young men whom Hana had never met before. Hana felt uneasy about this sway Nancy seemed to have with young men and wondered if this is what the Indian woman had meant.

After the holiday, things were quieter in the salon so Hana was not surprised when Najla told her that the agency had notified them that another placement had been finalised.

'You have been a good worker but the other girl is coming back soon. She had her first trip back after three years,' and Hana's heart missed a beat as she prayed it would not be that long until she saw Alim and her family in Mindanao again.

Whether it was because she was going or for some other reason, things were still in the room next door for the next few nights and Nancy invited her for sightseeing. Al Shams was much bigger than Cotabato and because she had often worked in the evenings or had no companion, she knew little of her surroundings. They visited the zoo. Nancy knew her way around there well. She must have been there before. They looked in shop windows in expensive commercial areas but Hana, who was repaying agency fees, bought nothing.

On her last evening, they met two other Filipinas who were working at the other tourist hotel in the town. One was very withdrawn and seemed troubled. She barely spoke all night. The other was a lot like Nancy, a bubbly personality with plenty of stories to shock and delight her other friends. They went to an ice cream parlour where some local boys called across from another table and laughed.

'Want to come for a ride in our car?'

Hana put her head down and was mortified to hear the bubbly personality agree.

'No! You can't! You don't know them, do you?' Hana gasped.

The others looked at her and the conversation became stilted. She wished she had not said anything because the rest of the evening became laboured and she was glad to be dropped off at Sandoz for her last night. Nancy went out again and she didn't hear her come in again.

Next morning Hana was woken by a loud knocking somewhere downstairs. It took her a few minutes to pull on clothes and still in a sleepy daze, to stumble down to the ground floor.

Two men were waiting at the side entrance. One was from the

agency. The other, dressed in a white *kandourah* and *gutra*, was a local man. One was as short and plump as the other was tall and sleek, one chattering, the other silent.

They greeted each other with the Arabic salutation which knew few boundaries. Then, 'Hello, miss! So you are now to move to your regular appointment just as we told you. The manager was happy with your work here and perhaps you could have stayed but you were only filling in. You knew that anyway, didn't you? Now you will be going as a housemaid for a family, just as you wanted, so you will be pleased and you will still do a good job. Now, this is your new employer,' and he called him by his name.

Hana was fully awake by now, surprised that this was happening so quickly, but then there were few formalities in her life here.

'He has come to drive you to the house where you will be working. This will be another emirate for you, so you have been lucky – three emirates in three months. Your new town is different from Dhahabi and Al Shams but people are friendly there. It is smaller but it will be good for you because you come from a small town too, don't you? There are other Filipinas there too so you will have plenty of company. Your employer speaks English so he will explain everything. We have arranged the necessary paperwork but if you need to clear anything, just contact us,' and he handed her a card written in English with Arabic on the reverse side.

It all happened so quickly that there was little time for goodbyes. Nancy came down and seemed genuinely sad that she was going. Najla kissed her several times on both cheeks and Hana glanced towards the vehicle which was to take her to Ras Al Jebel. The name meant 'peak of the mountain' and Hana would come to love the rugged, rock mountains of this coastal emirate.

The windows of the large four-wheel drive landcruiser were tinted and she could barely make out the figure sitting in the back seat. It appeared to be a woman whose head and face were covered in black material. Beside her was a little boy about six years old. In the front seat next to the driver was another child, older but perhaps not long out of primary school.

Hana was directed to the very back seat behind the woman, who also greeted her in Arabic. She would later find out that she was to work in a typical extended family which did not have the oil wealth of many families in the larger cities.

The driver of the landcruiser was the second of four sons, all of whom were married. The eldest worked in Abu Sharika and returned home to his family every fortnight. His wife and children lived in a compound near where Hana was to work. The second and third sons lived with their families in one compound owned by their father, now an old man who appeared to be well into his sixties. The woman in front of Hana was the old man's second wife, herself a woman in her fifties. The older of the two children was her son.

The man looked at her through the rear-vision mirror. 'Do you speak Arabic?'

'Just a few words and some sentences I can use in the house.'

'The women in the house speak a few words of English but they can understand some, so you will be all right. My sister speaks English. She studies. We have had housemaids before and they got by.'

They were out of the town by now and were travelling back along the road to the city with the sand dunes which had seemed so beautiful a few months earlier. Camels wandered along the roadside.

'The women will tell you what they want in the house. We have a driver and a man who looks after the garden. He also attends to our goats and chickens. You will be inside, mainly cooking and cleaning. Sometimes you will have to care for the little children. Do you like children?' He looked at her again through the mirror.

After some time they turned off the main road onto another well made but poorly marked highway. He asked her name.

They were silent again until the other woman spoke. The conversation became excited and Hana wondered what was happening as they started to shout. This subsided and the monotony and peacefulness of the surrounding desert enveloped the people in the car.

They passed a new road under construction and then out of the emptiness before them rose a town dominated by a huge roundabout with four roads running into it. The car stopped and the driver and the two boys jumped out.

A few minutes later, a young Indian came to the car with a shallow cardboard box in which there were two plastic cups filled with hot water and a floating teabag. '*Suliemani chai*?' he asked.

The woman nodded and he took the container of milk away. The tea had already been sweetened. Hana sipped it with satisfaction and looked around the square. She saw no other women and was grateful for the tinted windows. Whether or not they gave the women inside true invisibility, the effect was just the same. Curious eyes were unwelcome.

Although the hot weather had not descended yet, the square gave a feeling of heat. There were no trees here, unlike Al Shams, and there was no greenery except for the painted petrol bowsers at the filling station near the farthest end of the roundabout. There were still pools of water lying about after January rains. Evaporation was strangely low at this time of year. Scaffolding around the building sites at various points around the square gave a general sense of disorder.

The young man reappeared with a box of orange cream biscuits which he handed to Hana, who in turn handed them to the woman in front. Her name was Asma. She spoke a few words to Hana through the black chiffon which covered her face. As she did so, the cloth stuck to her lips. This type of cover was strange to Hana as Muslims in Mindanao did not cover in this way, yet in this all-male environment, Hana envied the woman her privacy even if it was behind a gauze veil. As months went by, the cover became more natural to her but she continued to find the mask which some of the older women wore in public intimidating in some way. These masks which came down over the nose and covered the mouth, giving the wearer an ugliness to frighten men away rather than entice them the way black chiffon face veils did.

The boys ran back to the car obviously more refreshed than the women inside, and jumped in noisily. The driver appeared, threw a glance to Hana asking how she was feeling and turned the ignition key. He barely spoke again except to point out some landmark here and there along the way.

While the first hour of the journey from Al Shams had been through sandy desert and dunes, the rest of the journey, the same length again, was through rocky desert, mountains and gorges – landscapes Hana had never seen before. She felt dwarfed by the cliffs rising in front of them at various points and was surprised when the road straightened out and turned into meadows and green fields, for the heavy rains on the more fertile land of Ras Al Jebel meant that this was the most natural agricultural region in the country.

As the landcruiser pulled to a halt outside heavy double gates opened by a man who could have been from anywhere on the Indian subcontinent, several children ran down the front steps of the house.

'Baba, you took so long!' they shouted in Arabic and then stopped again looking at her curiously.

'Why does she have a scarf on? Is she Muslim?' one of them asked.

The father nodded and opened the back doors of the car. 'You'll use the side door when you want to come in and out but we don't expect you will have any visitors unless you ask us first. You understand this is a family home.'

He opened the door and she followed him into a tiny passageway leading to a small room which was to be hers. There was barely enough room for the two of them to move around and it was something about their proximity which suddenly made Hana feel uncomfortable. She went to move out.

'Come here,' he called and he showed her the bathroom, another small room with a shower at one end and a squat toilet such as she was used to. 'It's not big but I'm sure you can make it nice. I'll get you anything you want in here so just let me know what sort of things you like. I've put carpet on the floor out here because there was some left over from the children's bedrooms and I thought I could use it up. You can eat in the kitchen or the breakfast room in the main part of the house. Sometimes the real driver,' he gave a laugh, 'or gardener will join you. I picked you up today because I like to meet people who are going to live in our house. I'm sure you'll feel part of the family after a while and you should feel comfortable with us.'

He moved closer to her and she knew she had to get used to different customs again for she had really had little exposure to men in the two months she had been in the country.

There was a call from a mosque nearby.

'Come! I'll show you the kitchen and you can meet the women,' and he brushed past her into the passageway again.

# Discovery

# 6

# March 1999

A grey wader with long legs and a thin, curved beak swooped on a tiny mouse. It flew to a small fishing boat nearby and played with its catch. Overhead, birds flew in formation. They would soon be returning to Russia, Oscar had told her. She watched little ground birds with crests which made them seem royal as they strutted about on the Corniche walkway. There were few people here so early in the morning – a lone fisherman or two, a Western woman walking in the early morning cool air and a man on a bike obviously keen to ride along the water's edge unhindered by the few cars, moving to and from the market.

The pale pink which had tinged the clouds had gone now and in its place a soft silver filtered through. The birds on the marshland beyond called out in as many voices as there were languages in this country. Migrants too, most of them, preparing to return to their homes, just like the workers. Hana smiled. She felt hopeful again thinking she was really like a bird.

She looked at her watch and wondered how much longer Oscar would be. He had asked her if she wanted to come with him to the early morning Abra Market. He had shown her the *abras* moored alongside the Corniche. He pointed out the Iranian boats which were the making of what they called the Iranian bazaar. Here you could buy anything from brooms to delicate tea sets called *estikan*. She saw the bales of stock feed for the animals, stored at this time of the year for the hot summer months when there was less growth. Trucks piled high with boxes of fruit and vegetables, much of it imported from India, Iran and Lebanon, were thrown deftly to the stall holders below, waiting to replenish their stocks. It was a small market, and clean, with little more than a high iron roof to protect people and produce in turn against the burning rays for half the year and the torrents which fell, often unexpectedly, in the cooler months. This year they had had continuous rain for two weeks, and with the floods, many people had left their homes.

Oscar was the Sri Lankan driver at her new workplace. He had suggested she walk along the Corniche while he went to see his friends who had been out on the early morning fishing boats. She enjoyed this time alone and her thoughts were far away when the cyclist came up behind her and squeezed a large handful of her buttocks before he furiously cycled off.

Just as furiously, though more with anger and indignity, Hana shouted after him in Tagalog, 'Where's your respect? I'm a Muslim woman! You wait! You wait!' She realised she was screaming now and wondered at herself. She felt alone but angrily bent and picked up three small stones. Would she really throw them or was this her way of arming herself against the roaming male who saw women alone as objects of their fun and pleasure. She squeezed the stones hard in her hand as she stormed along the pathway.

Lost in her thoughts and forgetful of time, she had walked further than she intended. She stopped and turned around, relaxing her grip on the stones. She looked at them. One white and smooth, another red embedded in pale grey, and the third black and sharp. These stones were talking to her, she knew that, but right now she could not hear them but she knew she would. She held them in her hand until she saw Oscar waiting by the car and she put them in her pocket. Somehow they were a sign to her that she should stand up for herself and learn to survive in this environment so different from her own.

'Where did you get to? I was worried that you might not come back,' Oscar joked.

Hana climbed in the back of the car, the runabout car they called it, and slammed the door hard.

'What's wrong?' he asked more gently. 'You were happy enough before.'

'Nothing!' She hesitated. How could she find the words within the English she had to explain the indignity still simmering in her.

'Something happened there, didn't it? Look, you'll get used to this place.' He wasn't sure if she understood but went on anyway. 'Maybe it was because you were by yourself and you're a woman and...' he turned back and looked at her clothes.

Hana knew what he meant. She had worn jeans and a T-shirt this morning because they were only going to the vegetable market. That had been a mistake, because she knew many of the men were staring at her. Maybe she should only wear these things in the house or perhaps she should keep to her own long skirts and blouses. She was used to that at home anyway. It was her Manila friends who made her forget that.

As they drove into the driveway, Al Rajul walked to meet them. In a not unfriendly way, he asked where they had been, looking at his gold plated diver's watch as he did. 'The women are waiting for you. It is better to tell them if you are going out because they have things for you to do.'

Hana understood and muttered her apology. She helped carry the vegetables into the kitchen, washed her hands and knocked on the adjoining door.

'Come in,' a woman's voice called in English.

An attractive young woman sat by the window. The long hair, loose over her shoulders, was still wet. She had just showered. The woman told her she was Asma's youngest daughter. She was not married yet and was a student at the women's college on the edge of town. She spoke English fluently. Her teachers were British, Canadian and Australian, she said. She asked Hana if she spoke Arabic. Hana knew life would be much easier if she could.

'Don't worry. I am often here so I can help if there are any problems,' and she told Hana that there were many Filipino women working in the canteen at the college where she studied.

'Do you want to dry my hair?' the woman asked, handing Hana the electric blow dryer. As Hana had seen this done plenty of times at Sandoz, she could easily oblige.

After a few minutes another woman walked in and spoke sharply to the younger woman.

'All right, all right,' she responded in English. 'That's enough now, *shukran*.' She listened as the older woman explained what Hana would be required to do each day and repeated it slowly to Hana. 'Come on. I'll show you around and you can see where you have to work.'

The duties were more or less what she had expected. Cleaning and cooking would keep her busy but they told her another cleaner from the Ben Majid Hotel came in once a month to go through the houses thoroughly. There was another house in the compound where the father and his second wife, her mother, Asma lived. A pathway joined the two houses but at present the maid's quarters of that house were empty.

'Most of your work will be with the children but sometimes you might have to do some things for my father. He's an old man now. This morning you are to clean his rooms because the other cleaner has already done our house.'

For a while Hana was so intent on her work that she lost track of the time. Then a car pulled up and the son went out to meet the father. From a side window Hana saw Oscar open the door for the old man who had been to check a new racing camel. A short while after, the kitchen door opened. The old man spoke in Arabic and then in English. He headed straight for Hana, who was alone now, muttering how good it was that someone had come to look after him again.

Hana found it difficult to respond to this open friendliness of the old man demanding her attention, for it was layered at the same time with a sternness which intimidated her. He looked much older than any other man she had known and may have been, because one of her grandfathers had died young. The other she had never known for he lived in Sabah. This man had a thick beard, more white than grey now but his eyebrows were still dark. She could remember that. They almost met in the middle.

He asked many questions, some in Arabic, some English. He knew a few phrases of Tagalog. This surprised the young worker, who had been washing freshly slaughtered chickens for the afternoon meal.

A patriarch, she was thinking, as his youngest daughter appeared in the kitchen from the front section of the house. His daughter noticed the young woman's efforts to listen and please and prepare the meal at the same time. With barely a hint of annoyance, she retrieved Hana from her father's attention and asked her to go back to her half-brother's house to help with the children. As she did, Hana put her hand into her pocket, puzzled by the weight. She felt the stones she had picked up on her morning walk and they strengthened her then as they did many times during the following weeks.


It was April. The clouds broke. These were very late rains. She watched the silver sheet stream from the narrow pencil window at the top of the stairs. They had talked of these rains, heavier than the desert had seen since the old men were little boys. That was before television, computers, electricity, water tapped into houses, and before schools and supermarkets had come to this northern emirate. That was before loudspeakers were attached to mosques. That was before the dual-lane highways, the airport and the factories. There had been big changes here but Ras Al Jebel still had the feel of a poor town.

As the children squealed below her, Hana looked down to see the two youngest in the family with their cousins who lived across the street running through the downpour.

'Come in, come inside!' and she scampered down the stairs barefooted. 'Don't be bad. Come in. You are wet.'

She pulled at the littlest boy. He struggled and laughed with the others. Her dress, soaked now, clung to her, outlining the firmness of the young body which showed she was a woman.

She was suddenly aware of another person on the veranda.

The grandfather laughed with his issue. He caught the other hand of the boy and joined Hana on the lower step. 'You are wet too,' he smiled as the last of the children skipped past them. 'You should come to my house and get dry.'

She returned the smile and put her head down, making to walk past him.

'No, come with me,' he said, blocking her way.

Feeling less a woman now, she stepped back, awkward and angry. A trapped animal, that's what she was, like a goat penned in a cavern with a sheer rock-face behind it.

'Father!' the daughter called from the passageway behind him.

Hana blushed as if she had been caught fingering the jewellery of the women of the house. She sensed disapproval and hurried as the old man stepped into the darkness.

'Hana, you come with me. Oscar will drive me to afternoon classes and I need a companion in the car. Go and get changed,' and she too looked at the firm body, younger than her own.

As she ran through the house leaving wet footprints on the ceramic tiles, Hana heard the women in another part of the house remonstrating with their offspring.

Once in her room, she pulled the wet clothes off with some effort and turned to close the door left open in her hurry. The children's grandfather stood there. Ferociously she slammed it and then wished it had not been done so loudly.

Her heart was beating furiously by the time she reached the car and even Oscar recognised the anger in her silence.

'Something has happened again? You were happy a while ago. What has made you angry?'

'Ask me later,' she hissed as she climbed in beside him.

He looked at the dress, deep blue and green, cut long and loose in local style. It had silver embroidery around the cuffs. She was very pretty, he thought, and kind.

Her eyes were green but now they flashed black, frozen into a frown. He had noticed that she did not wear jeans these days and he felt relieved. She had never told him but he guessed something had happened that first day on the Corniche. It often did when women were alone. Maybe like local women, she felt protected when she was covered up. Anyway, she was a Muslim, so what was the difference? She was different, though, he knew that. He had been to the Red Lion Nightclub at the Ben Majid Hotel and had seen the Filipino band. The girls who sang there wore short skirts, boots and chain belts – very tempting dress for these parts. In contrast, the waitresses in the coffee shop there were dowdy. They seemed to come from two different worlds and certainly two different generations. The Filipinas in many of the shops around town wore jeans, whether they were men or women, though in some places Filipino Muslims wore headscarves and long dresses as Hana did more and more these days. He had never been into the college where the girl of the house studied but the Indian cleaners told him of the workers in the canteen who wore jeans and T-shirts. He liked them, though. These people were friendly.

The brakes slammed sharply at the roundabout as a car screeched across in front of them. He liked the drive out here away from the city but he had to be careful of the goats, donkeys and camels which often strayed along the road from surrounding farms and pens. The times when Hana came with him were enjoyable because he knew he could take the long way back and they could spend some time alone. He liked to have women round him.

The security guards at the college waved as they pulled the heavy gates aside. Taxi drivers waved to him too. Many of them knew each other from around town. It was such a small place and little went unnoticed. One winked, seeing Hana in the front next to him. She turned away and sighed audibly. These responses tired her here.

Students moved in through the side gate. All wore black *abayas* which covered brightly coloured and often modern gear beneath. All of them had their hair covered and many their faces covered as well. She envied them their learning. They stepped delicately around and through puddles of water which reflected the mountains on the other side of the fence. Their shoes – Italian shoes – were too high and fragile for the stony desert ground, gold buckles and suede incongruous in the mud, dust and pebbles.

It was a hard place for men on their own, especially as so many of them earned too little to bring wives and family with them.

'We could buy an ice cream and eat it on the Corniche if you like,' Oscar said after the woman had left them.

'We should go back.'

'Just a little while.'

'It might rain again.'

'That's why it is good. No one will be there. Come on.'

It had been one of the few pleasures in the short time she had been there. This morning she had been particularly happy because she had heard from Rita the day before. She was coming to Ras Al Jebel for a while. This was doubly sweet as it had been unexpected. She had felt light-hearted but tensed again at the thought of the old man's eyes watching her.

Oscar wanted to touch her hand but wouldn't.

She shivered involuntarily.

'If you're cold we can go back.'

'No, but I'd like tea not ice cream,' and she told him about the letter from Rita. She wondered why she had not told him about the one she had received from Alim the day before. She had been happy to open it. Oscar was her only close friend in Ras Al Jebel – very like Alim the way they shared most things. She found she could not tell him everything, though. She was fearful of losing him. People changed their minds so quickly about others here. Goodness seemed a surface thing.

She wrote to both of them that night – a postcard to Alim and a letter to Rita but the messages in them both were different.

*April 1999*
*Ras Al Jebel*
*Dear Rita,*
*We have been here nine months this week. From your letter, everything*

*seems all right for you but I need to talk with you. I feel I have wasted my time. I have not made any money to send home yet but it shouldn't take too many months more.*

*I have had an interesting time in some ways but this is too different from Cotabatu or even Manila. It is so different from our way. The men and the women are different in their ways. The women do not work in the society like our women in Mindanao, even though it is a rural area. Perhaps this is wealth that does it but I think it is also poverty. We are rich because our women are side by side with our men.*

She wondered if the last line was true but knew that Rita would correct her if she was wrong.

*I have had some problems I will talk about with you. I thought I would fit in easily because I am Muslim too but that is not so in this family. The women are nice enough to me but I work hard. Sometimes they ask so many questions about my life and what I do and what I have done. The best time is when I go to the embassy with Mrs Asma or her daughter. Sometimes they do some activity there or go to a party, so I meet other Filipinas who are house-workers too. Some Filipinas work there as swimming teachers.*

*Sometimes the women in the house seem annoyed with me when I talk with the men, especially their men. I can't help that because the old man asks me to do things for him too. That is my job as well. I try not to displease them.*

*I don't have any real friends here yet except one person at my house. He is kind to me. The daughter in this house is at college but she is worried because her father has told her that if she does not pass her course she must marry her cousin, I feel sorry for her because this was what my father wanted me to do too. When she becomes worried with her work, she is cross with me. I understand why. Life is not easy for her. Her sister-in-law and her mother do not understand about college but they want her to succeed because they did not have such a chance. What can they do in front of their father-in-law and husband? He is an old man and they respect him.*

*I have heard some Filipinas here become Muslims. That is very interesting for me and different from home, isn't it. I look forward to seeing you. I don't know how you managed to change to Ras Al Jebel in such a short time. I hope you can stay. Tell me more when you write. They don't like me to phone much here. They say it wastes time. Phone cards are so expensive and I don't like to ring from the main street. Only men do that here.*

*Please write. I hope you can come here soon.*

She finished with the traditional Tagalog farewell and recognised that her own national language was still much better than her English, which had improved by talking with Oscar. How much more she was recognising through the language of the eyes and unspoken words of desire and affection, though, she now knew more keenly than ever.

# 7

# June 1999

She liked writing, though she had little chance or encouragement to do it. On quiet evenings she wrote poems about her feelings, this desert country and her longing for home and her family. Each week she wrote a letter or postcard to Rita, Alim or her mother. There was so much to say, so much that was new, although her life was the same day after day. She was sure that if she worked hard enough and long enough in this country, she could go back to study some day. Then, she knew, her writing would be put to a definite purpose.

*June 1999*
  *Ras Al Jebel*
  *Dear Rita,*
    *There is going to be a wedding in this house. What a change there is here! Remember when I wrote several weeks ago, I told you about Asma's daughter who is studying? Well, I think she did not pass her course in second term because I heard her mother and father arguing about some exams she could try again because she did not get enough marks. She still did not succeed and the people at the college said she must wait until next year and take the course again. The father says enough is enough. No man will want her with all this study and she should be a wife and mother now. She is getting too old. She is nearly twenty-one. Her mother has agreed. I don't know why, because she did not want this, I know. It's like us, isn't it?*
    *They have started preparing already. A huge red tent bigger than the size of one of our mosques at home, bigger than the mayor's house in Cotabato*

*even, has been set up down the road at the boy's house. Oscar showed me yesterday when we went for the vegetables. In our garden they have put up a smaller red and white tent but it is still as long as this house. They have already put huge carpets on the ground and are bringing in tables and chairs. I met an Iranian woman who works at the wedding catering company. She showed me photos of the decorations Asma has chosen for her daughter's wedding and for the henna painting ceremony a few days before. They are going to build a fancy stage to look like two thrones all covered in white satin and golden ribbons and bows. You can't believe it – it is so glamorous. The father wants some little fountains near the stage and cages full of white pigeons. Tables and chairs will be brought in. These will be decorated in blue, gold and white.*

*The henna painting party will be held outside – just for the women. A smaller stage decorated in green and gold is to be built. It is not such an important party, so they can make this one smaller.*

*The Iranian lady told me that the decorations, the tents and the stages will cost over forty thousand dirhams! Can you believe it? The lights decorating the tents will cost more and on top of this they have to order the food for all the celebrations. I can't imagine why anyone would spend so much on weddings. In this way, the customs here are very different from ours, even for Muslims like me. We have prayers, new clothes and plenty of food and even some dancing but not this.*

*Fereshteh, my Iranian friend, is very cheerful. There are many Iranians here. Some have lived here for years ever since their grandfathers settled. Other men come back and forwards on their boats. Fereshteh even says there are some people here without visas and they will be deported if they are caught. Fereshteh talks a lot about the families she has met through her wedding business.*

*My English is becoming better every day now, even though I'm practising and learning from Sri Lankans, Iranians and nationals. I haven't spoken to one real English speaker since I've been here, though I have seen some women once or twice at the market or in town.*

*Another company will prepare the food for the wedding, so I won't have much to do. Probably I'll help with the washing up. I don't mind, because it will be fun watching these things happening.*

*Oscar told me that at the men's part of the celebration, the men do their traditional dancing and shoot guns. He said that in some celebrations, the men get in their landcruisers and drive round and round in circles before they shoot. Maybe the car fumes affect them, he says.*

*If you are not here by the wedding day, I shall write and tell you all about it. I hope your life is good, Rita. We shall see each other soon.*

*Always I am your good friend,*

*Love to you,*

*Hana*

None of the stories Hana had been told about the wedding costumes could have prepared her for what she saw in the women's rooms. The dresses were out of a fairy tale book and were far from traditional Arab costumes. There were dresses for the henna painting party, dresses for each intervening day and a white wedding dress in an old-fashioned Western style, ready for the main celebration. It glimmered and glistened with sequins, glass beads, pearls and feathers. It was something from a movie set rather than a mere dress for a celebration. Even the shoes could have belonged to Cinderella – clear plastic, with feathers on the toes.

More than anything else that Hana would remember about the celebration was the magnificence of the flowers, though she was disappointed that the beautiful blooms had such little perfume, 'Because they mix plastic into them when they are growing,' Fereshteh told the unbelieving girl. They were beautiful – roses, gladioli, tulips, chrysanthemums and carnations – gold, white and pink, flown in from the Netherlands and South Africa, fresh for the occasion each day of the wedding celebrations.

Oscar gave a running report on the men's gathering and she found that celebrations there were just as lavish. Local musicians and bands made up of other Arab expatriates, and in some cases Pakistanis, all performing raucously in the men's tent, with a smaller but just as noisy group for the women. As well, the men had recorded music and a flashing disco arrangement with its own disc jockey, incongruous in the desert setting but in tune with the tastes of the flashy young Arabs who knew cars and had travelled.

Weddings here were noisy and joyous affairs, at least Hana thought so, and she was happy for Asma's daughter, herself now as radiant as her sparkling dress. At the same time, there was what appeared to be a calm resignation to an arrangement which was as old as the silent mountains shadowing them. She marvelled at the change in the young woman who had previously abandoned the idea of looming marriage in the face of study opportunities and yet now accepted her fate and the honour bestowed on her. Maybe it would not be the end. These days, more women were able to continue with their study after marriage and during child-raising. Though some like this family were wealthier, a certain degree of poverty still distinguished these northern people from those in the capital.

Everyone seemed in a good mood that final day of the wedding. Hana was infected with the spirit too. Asma had insisted on new clothes, so Hana too wore a long, traditionally cut dress in deep peacock blue. Her hair was tied back with a satin ribbon and her eyes sparkled.

Oscar, who spent most of the day with the celebrating men, raced in and out with new bouquets of flowers from well-wishers. Intoxicated by the merrymaking and captivated by Hana's glow that morning, he bent and kissed her hand as she took another bucket of flowers from him.

'Don't!' she whispered, though the light in her eyes belied her words.

He kissed her cheek and the warmth awakened something deep within her. His eyes were black now and he was short of words.

She looked at him with eyes which seemed to have caught every element of light in the shaded kitchen. There was no sound she could hear except for his breathy plea.

'Does it matter that I'm not a Muslim?' He knew it did.

She wished it did not, conscious only of being female and he male at that instant. He did not touch her again for she had gone pale. He was also caught in the wave of desire which had blanketed them both. She felt the other young woman's anticipation and envied her. To experience this thing with Oscar was all she could think of.

The door from the main part of the house opened. The effect was like a fluorescent light bursting onto a candlelit room or of raucous television voices drowning out the peaceful sounds of the desert in the late night. As ground birds would flee and crickets cease their complacent chattering, so the shock of that moment made Hana feel nauseous. This time her pale colour came from being discovered in the midst of a forbidden emotion – *haram* for a young woman outside her own.

The old man entered with his son, the half brother of the bride. There was an awkward silence – only for a split second – but all registered it. Oscar turned and moved quickly back out into the sunlight while Hana turned the tap to fill the bucket of flowers. The son, her master, followed Oscar into the garden and headed for the women's celebration. There was some message he had to deliver. Perhaps it was time for the bride to join her new husband, or perhaps more food had to be delivered, or some other detail for this wedding which should be perfect had been left undone.

The other man stood looking at Hana. He seemed younger today and Hana noticed that he actually stood tall. He rubbed his left hand against his loins, slowly, more slowly, lingering, a touch of tenderness as one would stroke a kitten.

Hana looked away suddenly confused. She turned for the door.

'Stop! Come here,' he said in a thick voice which seemed to come from his belly.

She wondered if he dyed his beard for the wedding. It had less grey than she had remembered from before. He caught her by the shoulders and bent down, trying to kiss her lips.

'Please, I must go,' she pleaded, aware of offending two masters.

As she did so, he fastened hot, slack lips on her. Feeling his tongue roused a strength in her she did not know she possessed. She pulled away.

The back door opened and just as quickly he had moved to the adjoining room. The third person could see only the shivering girl but not the forceful erection and determined eyes of the older man.

For the second time that morning, Hana's master looked at her knowingly.

In all places children believe in mythical people, legendary heroes and fairy tales of sorts. At some point they learn these stories are not true, the characters mere fiction and if it happens to them too early, their lives seem as if they are falling apart. So too the effect on Hana of all that had happened in that flash of time in the wedding celebrations. Her happiness with the wedding, the glamour, the women's enjoyment and Oscar's display of affection were shattered like a mirror destroyed in an angry bout of temper. An inner life had been so fragile and emotions too sorely tested that morning. She escaped to her room, more a shell than abode of comfort, closed the door and sobbed – racking, noiseless cries of anger and frustration.

Fereshteh listened sympathetically. The culture was like her own but then the life of poor women seemed the same in any country as far as she could tell.

Hana told her of her father's wish for her to marry Gammal. She talked of her friend Alim who understood everything so well – her friend who wrote and told her of the daily happenings around Quiapo, of the sufferings of their people and his belief that they could live good lives if they could change the mind of government. Fereshteh put her arm around the weeping girl who talked about her new friend Oscar.

'Hana *jan*. You are lonely and you don't have enough friends. You shouldn't let yourself fall in love with Oscar. It doesn't matter that he is from another country. That's all right in our religion but probably your family would not be happy that he is not Muslim.'

'But he's a Christian – a person of the book, so we have some things in common.'

It was true in fact that Oscar was somewhat of an anomaly in his own country and among his own people here, for he was neither Buddhist, Hindu or Muslim but part of the small Christian minority in Sri Lanka. He was an Anglican but that meant little to Hana, unused to the ways and religion of the British.

'You should try to spend more time with my family. I'll teach you some of the decorations you like so much. I can teach you special flower arrangements and, if you want to help on your spare day, we can have more fun together. Soon you will find other friends here too.'

This did not change all that had happened but it gave the girl new energy. She could also look forward to Rita's arrival in Ras Al Jebel any day. Things would be better in time. She did not talk about the old man, though. Somehow she felt guilty about his barrage of attention as though she had brought it on herself.

# 8

# July 1999

The phone rang. It was a local call.

'Your friend is here. She wants to see you. I told her she could come over this afternoon when we are resting because you will be looking after the little children when they come back from school.'

Nothing could spoil her day now – nothing. She had waited so long it seemed – almost half a year but now she was here.

On one hand, the fruits of leaving home were beginning to show themselves. After an initial down payment on the fees which the agency had paid for her, she was able to save money – a little but enough to send it home by bank cheque which she bought from the exchange in town. She had been so proud that day, and doing without small pleasures and delicacies was worth the satisfaction she felt able to provide for her own family. She had been frugal in her diet. Meals did not come with the job and she asked for no more in her room than had been provided in the beginning. She was now worried that any extra comforts might be seen as gifts and she wanted no more than was her basic right. She laughed when she thought of rights. It was strange to talk like this. She seemed to have lost so many things she took for granted. She could not leave the job even if she wanted. There were debts to pay and she did not hold her passport until everything was returned. This was her sponsors' guarantee of her fidelity to his generosity in paying sponsorship fees for her. She could not complain, though. They were all in the same situation and today nothing would taint her meeting with Rita.

The old man watched as the two young women embraced, laughed and kissed each other. It irritated him. He knew these Filipinas were warm. He knew all about it. He had experienced it before when he travelled and he had heard stories. After all, his money was sponsoring the woman. The least she could do was be grateful. He must talk to his son. It was ridiculous that she spent so much time with his children. They should find another person for that. He needed her help in this house. There was plenty for her to do, especially now that his wife spent so much time with the other women. Their son was at boarding school and, with their two daughters married, she needed other company. Yes, they needed another servant in his son's house. Oscar would know someone for that. Another man would keep him out of mischief!

The truth was that Oscar was a challenge to the old man's manhood but he would never admit that. He was a strong man – he had plenty of children. Yes, that was it, he needed another wife. He needed relief. Asma was old and tired now.

He looked at the girls again, chatting in the sunlight and he moved on the cushions with some feeling of pleasure.

Hana's heart sank when she was told of the move. Oscar was just as unhappy about finding another worker for the son's kitchen. That was Hana's place but at the same time he knew of several Sri Lankans looking for employment and there was a young Pakistani at a local restaurant looking to supplement his thin salary.

He was worried about the old man. He knew his disposition without Hana voicing her concerns. Men knew these things but what could he do except tell her to be careful? He was not so sure of Hana's friendship that he could push her too hard. She might interpret it as jealousy. He might push her to someone else, even the old man, if he became too possessive. She was so serious and her life was narrow enough as it was. She did not need the pressure of his good advice to come across as criticism. What worried him more was that Asma suspected nothing, moving quite cheerfully between each house, and by spending more time with her married daughters and other women relatives, she was leaving the old man alone in the house with Hana more and more.

The tension for the two workers eased when the son and father left to oversee the family business in the capital. Two days passed and Hana began to feel that her concerns might have been of her own making. She had a sense of relief and at the same time began to feel remorse for what had gone before. She was glad she had not said too much to Rita and even more relieved that she had not mentioned her fears of the old man to Fereshteh, who was fast becoming a friend to the two Filipinas.

Rita had been relocated to Ras Al Jebel to work as a housemaid for a Pakistani doctor, a specialist in ear and throat conditions. He was based at the hospital near the women's college where Asma's daughter had studied before her marriage. Hana knew the hospital well as she had passed it many times when she had gone as company with Oscar and the student. Not only did she know the hospital but she knew friends of the doctor – her own Pakistani family from Al Shams. They came to visit a few weeks later and the group of friends met for a *kebab* picnic near the mineral springs on the edge of town. The waters were hot and a spa resort had been built where women had their own section and pool for relaxing.

In the warmth of the murky waters, Hana was invigorated in a way she not been since leaving the Philippines. It was not a luxurious place and the name of resort was rather grand for the simple building and tiled pool but it was a special place for Ras Al Jebel town, which could hardly boast that it was much more than a large rural village.

As the women relaxed, Hana told Rita in Tagalog about Alim's letters, Oscar's friendship and, at last, of the old man's unwelcome advances. 'It wasn't anything much, I suppose, but he should know better than to be like that if he is a good Muslim. I'm a Muslim woman too. He knows that, so why does he do this?'

'Be careful,' Rita warned. 'Here they say one thing and do another but if you are caught there can be trouble.'

'But I'm not doing anything. I just want to work and see my friends,' she protested. 'Anyway, it is peaceful now. The men are away.'

The peacefulness was short-lived. The carefree days were a brief respite and the men were back. Hana was now blossoming. She had been sleeping well and eating better though still very simply. She was happy to have her friends around her and this showed. There was a bounce in her step again and she welcomed the two men warmly when they disturbed her collecting washing from the side clothes line. The older man sat chatting, telling her of Abu Sharika and its sights. She had not seen it but believed the city was more beautiful than Dhahabi. The tree planting had given it more of a Mediterranean feel than Dhahabi, he said.

'You haven't been to the Mediterranean, have you?'

'No, this is the first country I've been to after my own.'

'You should come with me next time I go,' and he abruptly got up and walked inside the house. She folded the clothes and followed him with the basket balanced on her hip. He was standing by the door as she pushed it open. Without saying anything, he took the clothes, placed the basket on the floor and put his arms around her. 'Hana, I have wanted to see you very much.'

She knew she could be firm with him. After all, he was an old man. Maybe his mind was going. She wished his wife would come.

'How about a little kiss for a lonely man?'

'Please, your wife will be angry and I don't want to lose my job and...'

'Just warm me up,' he interrupted and held her close to him. Old man or not, he had a strength on which she had not reckoned.

'Someone's coming!'

There was no one but he was concerned enough to glance behind him, half expecting one of the women. The words between them suddenly took on the character of a game. She seemed to be teasing, urging but not reviling him. She did not know it but she was stirring a fire in the old man, standing tall now with a desire about to explode.

'Silly girl,' he breathed. 'I've given you this life and job here. You should be good to me. That's what you are here for.'

She ran back out into the yard, out of his grasp and stayed away from him for the rest of the day, arguing with herself about how she was dealing with his persistence.

He sulked like a child, probably more because his wife seemed to follow him around the house as much as anything else.

Hana knew she had to talk with Rita but the phone was not the answer. She would see her next day somehow. As it turned out, this was not possible because Asma decided to visit her daughter, back from the extended honeymoon in Malaysia. She left a list of things to do in her house.

'And you can clean my husband's study before he gets up!'

That would be the first thing on the list! Get the study cleaned and keep out of his way, she told herself.

She cleaned quickly, straightening here and there, wiping the soft cloth across polished surfaces and finally dragging the vacuum cleaner out of the cupboard in the passageway, annoyed that the room was carpeted. This meant he could hear her in there. She waited and wondered if she might leave the floor but could see that it needed attention. With heart beating now, she flicked the switch and might as well have called him.

She was taking the dust bag from the machine as he walked up behind her. She had not heard him cross the thick carpet in his bare feet. He lent over her bent figure, slim with the morning light behind it. His maleness pressed into her buttocks. He unbalanced her and walked over to his desk, picked up the ledger and moved away.

'Why are you always so nervous? You need a man,' and he sat in the armchair near the window. 'Relax!'

She did not speak as she picked up the pieces of the cleaner, spilling the dust as she did so. She clicked her tongue at her own clumsiness. Now she would have to spend more time cleaning up in front of him. When she returned with the dustpan and brush, he was standing again, clearly agitated.

'Young lady, I don't know why you don't like me. I really like you. I think you are very pretty. I think about you a lot,' and he stood in the doorway again so that she could not leave.

With heart beating, she stood some way off, then, suspecting this was to be a battle of wits, moved closer to make an exit. He stepped towards her and she backed into a corner, where he promptly put his hand on her shoulder and caught her other hand. He pushed it against an erection she did not recognize. He held it there as she struggled. She felt the hardness grow and throb.

She clenched her teeth and pinched him hard with her free hand. 'If you don't let me go, I'll scream and the women from the other house will hear me. Have some respect.'

'Have you ever felt a man as strong as this? You know you could make me happy,' and he pushed forward to kiss her neck, ears and mouth while she struggled and squirmed. 'Just like a naughty baby,' he laughed as the phone rang and he could hear his son leaving a message on the answering machine.

She waited for no more and bolted as he lifted the receiver and spoke brusquely. Permission or not, she had to see Rita.

The car was gone and she could not see Oscar. She ran from the front gate and turned the corner as a taxi slowed down next to her.

'Where are you going?' She recognised one of Oscar's friends. She promised to pay him later and asked him to take her to the Pakistani family.

'Hana, what are you doing here at this time?' the Pakistani woman called out from the garden where she was enjoying the last cool days before the heat rose from the desert again.

'Please, I need to see Rita,' she panted.

'She's about to go to town with me.'

She joined them, shaken and withdrawn now.

Rita knew immediately that something was seriously wrong. She did not seem surprised. It was as if she had heard it before. 'Do you think he might stop?'

Hana shook her head, dubious now of the old man's next move.

'I don't know. You could tell his son or the women but they will be angry. I'll come with you to Fereshteh's shop. She is from these parts and will have more of an idea what to do.'

Fereshteh had much to say. She had heard this story before and saw Hana as a lone creature caught in a furious and unpredictable desert storm. 'You can't keep on like this, Hana. It's not good. You have to understand the attitude of some of these men. If you tell the women, your life is going to be difficult. I don't think they will keep you, or else they will be suspicious,' the Iranian woman advised.

Hana did not understand the word but could sense its importance in the situation.

'Maybe you should talk with the people at the agency. It's their job to make sure you are doing a good job and that you are cared for.'

Again she felt trapped. She needed the job. She wanted to work. 'I want to stay. I don't care what they do. I still owe money and I have only sent a little bit home and my family are already very pleased,' but she also sensed a determination in the old man's wanderings. It seemed he was not so old after all. Many older men in her country bore children by younger wives. Even here, old men continued to take very young women as their third and fourth wives – poor rural girls bound by poverty and driven through compliance with family's wishes.

Permits and visas, debts and obligations, fear and indignation – her head spun. She felt weak and she remembered the relative innocence and simplicity of her life in Mindanao – a childhood where conflict and aggression were things which happened somewhere else. This was not in her nature, which had been formed in an open community, a nature which knew fun and frivolity but abhorred the force which was becoming commonplace in their society.

# 9

# August 1999

The plane took off slowly, gaining momentum when it was in line with the mountains still some way off. Then it suddenly soared into the crisp, near dawn sky, not yet faded by the haze of mid morning. Another smaller plane cut into the landscape, more like a single bird, the last of the season heading north to Russia again. It seemed strange to see such large planes coming and going from Ras Al Jebel airport. It always seemed empty and had the same feeling about it as many of the large shopping marts built around the town but which still stood unused many months later.

Appearances were important. Even Hana felt forgotten and unheeded in the big house where social life continued for the women as it had done for generations before. Today was one of the exceptions as she accompanied them to the airport to collect luggage sent on ahead by another son of the first marriage. She could hardly call the women her friends but she was often a companion for them.

They ordered coffee as they waited, not today the bitter golden coffee of their area, more cardamom than anything else. Here they had bigger cups of sugar sweetened Italian coffee. Hana did not enjoy it usually but as the women pressed it on her, she accommodated, caught up in the excitement of the trip.

Rita had laughingly told her that the foreigners working in the town went out to the airport for bacon sandwiches and the best cappuccino in town. Hana wondered what was so special about bacon sandwiches, though she had not eaten pork. Even in her home town where pigs wandered freely, pork was often served at celebrations and festivals that both Christians and Muslims attended.

Thursday was the busy day. Uzbekistan Airlines flew today. She wondered where Uzbekistan was, interested that several of the staff had that Chinese look about them, though she knew they were not.

She enjoyed outings with the women, even if they complained because she knew that their lives were as monotonous as her own and at least with them, she knew what to expect. The men rarely accompanied them on these occasions, so Oscar was the driver. For both of them, these were chances to be together even if there was little room for conversation.

She knew Oscar came out here each week or at least he said he was going to the airport. Sometimes he came back dishevelled and sweaty. She did not know why but thought of the fighters in Mindanao at these times. Even now as she walked near, he stopped talking and his demeanour seemed to change. What was it about Oscar, the man so kind to her and yet so distant?

The eyes of each woman followed two other female figures who had apparently been farewelling staff or the passengers of the plane now heading over the mountains. They were Russian, not big but voluptuous by any standards. Their hair hung loose, too fair to be real, but being uncovered was enough for the older woman to click her tongue.

'Shameful! They should cover here. It's bad for our men.'

The women continued talking and Hana had picked up enough Arabic to know that the conversation was about certain women around town who were being visited by men.

'At least our men would not go to these women,' the older one said.

Hana looked at them again and wondered. Then her gaze continued to the next table and she watched one man fingering his *tasbi*, so like the rosary Rita carried in her bag. This was one custom which the Muslim men in her country had not adopted. There was something about the movement of the beads through fingers which she found disconcerting.

One of the men caught her eyes watching them and smiled as she looked quickly away.

She thought about her life here again. It could go on this way for days and she liked it, liked the predictability, the sameness, the monotony even. Of course she was used to sameness – the sameness of tropical seasons which changed imperceptibly except for the hot season rains and the cooler months which they called winter. She had not experienced storms like desert storms, though, in spite of living near the sea.

At the same time, she knew that not far from her own home in Mindanao there was fury at work when army met rebels. Their men knew how to stand up against injustice. Here, the workers just grumbled and complained. They were without families. They had no women and there was little softness in their lives.

Some brown goats with matted coats wandered into the compound outside the restaurant. The woman pushed her cup towards Hana, who responded quickly, ordering a refill. She wandered past the frosted-glass partition, across to Oscar who was standing by the counter talking to a customs officer.

The swing door squeaked back and forth as men with two little boys entered. Hana recognised one of them, who smiled shyly across at her. She heard them tell the man in uniform that they had come to collect veterinary supplies – special tonics developed by Czech scientists.

'Can you carry this?' Oscar interrupted her thoughts as he slid the boxes across the floor.

She picked up the smallest one and struggled with it to the trolley, where it landed with a thud.

'Be careful! We don't know what's in it.'

She looked around the empty airport again and wondered if it was ever full. Most of the workers were foreigners like herself. Filipinas dozed behind the canteen counter. Indians took care of maintenance and electrical and plumbing problems. Lights flickered overhead as one changed a fluorescent bulb. Pukhtuns, hardened by the mountain winds, carried baggage to cargo planes, and thinner Indians, Bengalis and Sri Lankans who looked as if they would break beneath the loads hurried behind.

Each time she had been here, it had an aching, empty feeling as sad as a wedding without guests. The greyness suddenly depressed her. Why was it that the golden sands of the vast expanses seemed to stop as soon as they reached the towns in this country?

As if he could read her thoughts, Oscar told her to call the women and she went back more cheerily. They had told her that they would stop at the embassy in Khuzam today. This meant she would meet some other Filipinas working there or maybe some other visitors. She had met them before with Asma's daughter but had not seen them elsewhere since then.

They lived closer to the airport than the club, so Oscar dropped the luggage first. The women remained in the landcruiser while Hana helped carry the boxes to the foot of the front steps. She was curious to know what they contained but knew she would probably never find out. The other workers carried them up one by one – gingerly, as they were heavy. Oscar had taken his shoes off as he moved nimbly up the marble steps, short and modest enough in this house, though good Iranian marble just the same. It was translucent in the sun like the skin of old women hidden from sunlight for many years. A golden thread wove its way through and stood out like a protruding vein on a smooth temple.

Hana noticed some sand had blown out of the window boxes on either side of the steps. She brushed it aside with her foot, reminding herself to sweep it later when she arrived home again.

Oscar was the only man in the house she really liked. She knew he was attracted to her but he was gentle. She sensed he respected her wishes and would push no further than she wanted to go. This was not far, though. She heeded Fereshteh's advice, at least at this point, but she wanted his friendship and tried to indicate this as simply as she could from her confused feelings. She skipped to the vehicle again and was thankful she could climb in next to him. The women, with faces still covered, sat there mutely watching the activities.

As they drove into the built-up area near the embassy, the women behind her reminded Oscar to collect them in two hours' time. Then they would collect fresh bread from the *tanoor* and pastries from the new, modern Hot Bread Shop which brought a taste of Dhahabi's glamour to Ras Al Jebel. The gate opened and the guards waved in a semi-salute.

Because the women were not able or not prepared to walk far from the car – Hana could not decide which – the vehicle drove up close to the door of the beauty salon. She laughed to herself, remembering how she would have worked on the other side of the door several months ago. Her life had changed but not to the extent she had anticipated.

She waved to Oscar, saw the women through the door and hurried around the back of the kindergarten building with its sign 'Montessori School' where she knew other Filipinas would be working. The smallest child from her family came to classes here. His father had dropped him on his way to work while the women were still in the airport. She could hear their chatter and remembered again that she had wanted to be caring for children in this Gulf country but her duties had not worked out that way.

Other sounds came to her – music, laughter and a woman's voice issuing orders, exhausted and monotonous but with little authority. She went into another building, with its sign in English showing that this was the gymnasium, and sat on the bench at the back of the hall, draughty in its emptiness. A small group of young, mostly Middle Eastern women were dressed in exercise gear of various hues, cuts and styles. This was quite a contrast with the attire of the house and bore no relation at all to how women in the street appeared.

The exercise session stopped and women collected towels and made their way to the showers and sauna.

Emmi, the young instructor came over to Hana. 'You should join us next time.'

'I'm not of their class,' she answered in Tagalog.

They came from the same island so used a dialect which made Hana want to throw her arms around the other girl. There was no need to say any more. They understood their place and the role they played. They served the purpose for which they had been brought to this country and no one really cared about a social life for them at all.

'It's a pity the other one is married now because you could have been coming here more often. She used to do aerobics too, you know. Only the young ones are really keen and some of them can't bear to change. If they dressed more casually it wouldn't matter but it's such a big deal for them.' She picked up her own towel and pulled a sweatshirt over her head. 'Come and have some tea. The others might be there now.'

It was a strange complex – many rather plain prefabricated buildings sitting around a large central square like plastic houses on a Monopoly board. At one end there was another fence with a gate. Hana had seen the swimming pool before. Little children sometimes had lessons there but apparently the women seldom swam because the sun would burn them or – worse, apparently – tan them. The beauty parlour and kindergarten were at the other end and the gymnasium from where they had just come was on the third side. Between these and the main office block on the other side was a huge expanse of cement which seemed to glow white-hot in the summer season but which was grey like the sky around it today.

Several Filipinas were seated around a table in the canteen. As they approached, the conversation became more animated but the voices dropped even further.

'They will deport her if they find out.'

'That's not so bad as long as it's not worse. I have heard that in some emirates they use lashes on them.'

There was silence. Hana shivered. An unwanted pregnancy held close until discovery. Birth usually followed by punishment, particularly if the father was another worker. If he was a national, that was another story.

Hana had not wanted marriage, not with a cousin decided by her father, but in a flash she saw something peaceful, kind and gentle about a family life on her island, no matter how simple. She let the thought take her over while the other young women chirruped around her.

'Come here, Fatema!' one of them called out to a young woman who came in for coffee.

Fatema was unusual in Ras Al Jebel. She was one of the few local women to work and she had a dignity about her which Hana had seen in Asma's daughter. They had been friends and the last time Hana had seen her was at the wedding. She remembered and smiled at her. Perhaps it was the familial culture greeting the other. Fatema had been to the women's conference in Beijing with this small country's official delegation. Her severe exterior was like her *abaya*. It was external. She could put it on and off. Here she worked hard for the women at the centre, aware of its possibilities to help women move beyond domestication. She wanted more for them, more for the young women in front of her as well but she knew that changes, though inevitable once they got together, would follow a predictable pattern and in this society it would be slow.

She was to fight hard for Hana, though neither of them knew it yet. In her heart she knew that patriarchy affected so many people who stepped inside this culture, whether they were of it or not. It affected men and women, though in different ways. She had heard expatriate women complaining that their men changed here too. They liked to be kings, though they would never admit it. This patriarchy was not as primitive as the craving of the mother in women but it was a thirst which returned again and again in the alleys and along the highways of the journeying. It was something many men wanted but which made them a little less real, like sinking into quicksand with no room left to breathe.

Although Hana could not express this, she felt it. Oscar's maleness was different – a tenderness burning with a desire for justice. Though not one of them, he often talked of the Tamils and their fight and struggle in his country. Here in a monotonous land, so many struggles, so many arrows for one bow but heading for one target.

# The Judgement

# 10

# September 1999

The phone rang in Fatema's office. She lifted it lazily. Was this really all the job meant – language classes, aerobics and kindergarten?

'*As-salemu alaikum.*'

Fatema did not recognize the voice but detected an accent.

'My name is Fereshteh. You don't know me but we have heard about you and your work on the radio. We are friends of Hana.'

Fatema replied, fully awake now in spite of the heat. It was almost May and was hot. It would stay like this for many months, so many months that it seemed never ending. She heard noises in the background.

'Fatema, we are friends of Hana,' the woman repeated and she explained who she was. 'There is a terrible problem! We need to meet you today, quickly. Hana is in trouble and needs help.'

She sat up now, stimulated, as if this is why she existed. What sort of trouble, she had asked. They arranged to meet in half an hour. A man would be there too. Did she mind?

Alert now but concerned as well, she telephoned home and said she would not be there this afternoon. She had other work to do. They understood, though they could only guess in what she was involved now – an unwanted arranged marriage, a second wife, an ambitious student wanting further study or work, an errant husband? These were the problems of her women, and her father, trained in law, would support her through all of them, particularly when local families complained about her interference.

She stood near the gate in the shade of a peppercorn tree. The security men watched her intrigued. They rarely saw the young coordinator except as she came in and out of the back entrance driving her own car. She was obviously waiting for someone.

When the meeting did happen, it was more than they had expected. The combination was strange – a Middle Eastern woman in a scarf, Iranian possibly; a Filipina, though they did not recognise her; and a man, Sri Lankan or Indian, too small to be a Pakistani. Maybe a Bangladeshi, they could not be sure. They thought they could have seen him before but not with either of these women.

Fatema was just as curious and climbed into the car, still not sure of what had happened. It was past closing time but the man could not come into the building in any case.

They drove some distance in tense silence, apparently watching to see if they were being followed. Fatema sensed this was no ordinary problem.

'Do you mind if we go somewhere out of the way?' Fereshteh asked after the brief introductions had taken place. 'We need to talk privately where people won't see us.'

On the way, a brief outline of what they knew drew Fatema into the fog of tension.

'It's our friend Hana. You have met her at the club. It seems like she has killed someone.'

Fatema remembered the gentle woman and looked at the strained faces around her. She did not have to ask questions, for the story came out in rapid bursts like gunfire.

'The old man in the house where Hana works has been found dead. It looks like he was killed. They say Hana did it. She won't talk now but Oscar has more details.'

The woman was distressed and her face as much as her words pleaded with her. 'You know people. We have heard that your father is a lawyer. She needs help but we don't know how much it will cost or what we should do.'

It did not happen often but, when it did, Fatema knew she had connections she could use and she had the will to fight – to the end.

Oscar turned past the airport. He had the family's car but he knew that, when they missed it and could not find him, there would be trouble. For his sake, for Hana and for his friends, he could not afford to lose his position. A pick-up truck waited further down the road. The car stopped.

'I'll leave you here and try to get back but I must take the car to the house. Don't worry about these people. They are friends and will look after you.'

He left them with the two Filipino men. Rita sat beside the driver with the other women in the back seat. Through the small window behind them, they could see the second man in the tray behind, almost like a sentry. They drove about twenty minutes and turned down a side road, coming to a gate beyond which were rough buildings. It looked like a construction camp but there was no building site or excavation in this area.

'You'll be safe here,' the driver said, parking the truck. 'Just press the horn when you are ready to go.' He lit a cigarette as soon as he touched the ground and handed the packet to the other man.

The women watched them cross the compound and enter a building. As they looked around, they were aware that this was no ordinary camp. There were guards here too, though not in uniforms.

They brushed other questions aside in the urgency of the moment and told Fatema what they knew. Slowly she pieced the picture together. The story was disjointed and fragmentary – hearsay and put together from what they had known to be happening over the past few months.

She had come to Oscar's door, subdued, shocked and strangely calm – resigned perhaps, he was not sure, except that this was a different woman from the one he had seen the evening before. He had seen this calm before. He had seen it in the eyes of men who killed enemies. A calmness for justice done. He had always admired the rebel he thought he found in Hana but this he had not expected. A pale, haggard figure, she had not spoken at first. It was late. Because she was shy of their attraction, she would not have come like this normally.

He had not slept well because it was hot and something had disturbed him. The moon was not quite full. It looked as though the artist had run out of paint, unable to finish it, uneven and jagged along the edge. Maybe this was the reason he was restless, he thought, as he boiled his little kettle on the gas ring near the back door.

Shadows moved. Stray cats. There were plenty of them in this area. They lived among the containers placed at intervals along the road for the local community's rubbish. Rats and snakes too but it was an odd time for them to be moving.

He listened again. It was time he went back to his country. He cared for Hana but there was no chance here.

It was all the more surprising for him when she came to his door. She did not knock. She was just there, standing with the moonlight behind her, so bright that he thought he could see right through her. Her feet were bare and her dress was pulled in such a way that he knew she had dressed quickly.

'We want to see her. Oscar knows where she is but he says we have to have a plan first otherwise his idea is better. He wants to get her out of the country but that's impossible and it will look like she has done it if he does this. We can't believe that she would. That's why we need to talk with you. We need support as well as Hana.'

Fatema felt she was dreaming but it was more like a nightmare made worse by the heat even in this late afternoon, beating down on them in the truck.

'She told Oscar some things early this morning but not everything.'

Rita explained what had taken place a few days earlier, a problem which had been brewing for many months, perhaps chipping away all that time until the barrier between them had almost broken down. Both she and Fareshteh had known of it. She bit her lip. It was worse than she had imagined and Hana's resolve was tougher than she had dreamed.

Many weeks earlier she had been with Hana when she had telephoned the agency asking to move. She had spoken to the same man who had met her that first morning she had come to Ras Al Jebel from Al Shams.

'You know, one of the men from the agency told her not to be so sensitive. He said it wouldn't hurt her to give the man a kiss if he asked for it. He was only an old man, he said, harmless. It was just a kindness and she shouldn't make a big thing out of it. Hana argued with him. She said it wasn't like that. Can you believe it? We're supposed to be there to kiss these old geezers!' She had heard the word from her friend at the college, who had learnt it from one of the teachers who came to talk with them each day. It was a strange word but a good fit for the old man, she and Hana had agreed.

'She wanted to talk with Lucy.' Rita went on to explain how Lucy knew them all from their time in the Philippines. 'She was away visiting other workers on their six-month assessment visit so she didn't speak with her then but she did later. When she did get on to Lucy, she thought it was funny too. Maybe none of us took it seriously enough before.'

Before she could continue, the driver came back to the truck.

'We're going to pick up Oscar. You can come or you can wait here and have some food, because he might want to talk with you. There is a spare hut there,' he said, indicating. 'There aren't any men and no one will disturb you. The guards will make sure of that.'

So they were guards, the women thought, as they looked at the slouching figures in the shade.

'My boss knows what I'm doing so it's all right for me,' Rita replied.

The others nodded. They felt safe here although the setting was far from conventional. Fatema led the team as if she had been here before, confident now that this was her society and her role was crucial to the safety of Hana.

Once inside and sipping hot, black tea, Rita responded to Fatema's questioning.

'You see, Lucy finally came up here to visit the two of us and a couple of others who had been working here longer than us. They were due for their six month visit so it wasn't that she thought Hana's problem was very serious. The idea was that Lucy would visit us at our workplaces and talk with our employers as well. For the two of us, this meant she had to come to the houses. Hana told me that when she told Lucy about the old man annoying her, Lucy was sympathetic. Because his wife – second wife, you know,' the detail seemed important enough for Rita to emphasise it, 'because she was away, Lucy had to talk with the old man as well because he was the first boss. When he walked in, Lucy started to laugh. He was angry and so was Hana. He didn't know what they had been talking about but maybe he guessed because Lucy asked Hana in our language if this man had the energy. Hana was annoyed because she thought Lucy wasn't taking her seriously and she said she put her head down. Then Lucy told Hana he didn't have any teeth left so how could he get it to stand up. I made jokes and made Hana laugh about it too when she told me but the problem was it was, alive and still active or at least he wanted it to be.' She looked at the two women, knowing that she could have made them laugh if it was not so tragic.

'Sometimes he would play with himself so that Hana could see.' By now she knew, however, that what she and the others had dismissed as a senile man's fetishes were much more.

By now, Fereshteh was more worried. She feared for Hana.

'What have the police said about this?' Fatema asked finally.

'They want her for questioning because they say there is evidence that she knows what happened. Oscar says that means they think she did it.'

Fatema waited before she asked, 'Do you think she did?'

No one spoke.

A car pulled up close by. They heard men's voices outside before there was a knock on the door. Oscar waited for their reply before he walked in.

'Do you know where Hana is?' Fatema asked immediately.

'Yes, she's safe for now. What do you think will happen?'

'Well, we have to talk with her quickly.'

'Before you do, I think you need to go back to town, Rita, because your agency has sent Lucy up here. She is staying with a family we know and wants to see you. She will meet you at the embassy in an hour and a half if you agree. We don't want anyone to speak with Hana until there is a plan.' Again he mentioned the word 'plan' and Fatema wondered who he meant by 'we'.

'Please would you go back to see her and then we'll meet again tonight and decide what should happen. I'll ring you, Fereshteh, because there will be fewer questions that way.'

Oscar now seemed in control. He called the driver again and gave directions to the club as he was not to accompany them this time. He had been refused the use of the car by the family, distraught at their father's death. He had given some weak excuses about being out for the evening but this passed unnoticed in the midst of the grief.

The agency had been contacted early that morning. Lucy had called the embassy and had been sent up with orders to speak with the family and Hana if she could. The embassy was an easy place for her to start with the women, as she could get to it easily and need not attract much attention.

Oscar had made the arrangements once he knew she was coming. It was clear he knew much more than he was telling them. 'They have been complaining about Hana for a few weeks now. They say that she visits you too much, Rita.'

'That's not fair,' Rita protested. 'That man and his friends have been annoying her. I don't know exactly what he did last time she came but she wouldn't go back. She stayed overnight until they came to get her. My family is very good. They like Hana. They knew her before she came here. She refused to go back. I guessed it was too much kissing. Maybe you can find out. Would you believe that the next day a couple of the man's friends came over and told my boss that she had to go back.'

Rita remembered. It had not been one of their usual happy days. Hana was tense – a strange thing for someone from the southern Philippines, where singing, children and lazy conversation were part of everyday life, refreshing tired spirits like light showers after the build up of humidity.

'You see, lots of people were beginning to see that there was something wrong with Hana, or wrong with her home. She is a quiet person but not very quiet and your religion is hers too, so we thought it would be easier for her.'

It had been a harsh reaction, shaming Hana, insisting that she travel back in the car with the two men sent to fetch her, even the Filipinas recognised that.

The women talked longer but did not get much further. They needed to see Hana.

'What do you think will happen if she gives herself up to the police? No one knows for sure that she did it. It just looks that way,' Rita said hopefully.

Fatema did not voice her greatest fears. In some emirates she could be held indefinitely. These people were anonymous in the eyes of many. They came. They went. They knew the punishments for transgressing the law, or so the law said. Some became examples for others. This was her fear – extreme actions breeding reactions to mirror them.

Three women, aware to varying degrees of what had happened in the young Filipina's life, wondered what had really gone on. The reality of the law still had not dawned on two of them. It was a harsh environment. Laws could be applied vigorously. This was one way to maintain control. This was how they kept a semblance of order in this ancient land where traders, pirates and desert people made their own laws, laws which changed from day to day depending on the players, treaties and booty. Pardon and forgiveness in the hands of rulers, dictators and autocrats with reconciliation only from their hand as they saw fit – *diya,* their own form of justice.

# 11

# September 1999

'The police have been at the house all day. They have been asking questions about Hana and about me. I don't want to leave her but something has to be done or I am going to be implicated in this as well. I want to protect her but I can't see an easy way right now.' Oscar had lost his self-assurance in his plan.

'Oscar, I don't know what you are thinking and where Hana is right now but it's not going to work. If she did kill the old man, there must be a reason. She needs help whatever way it turns out. If you hide her, she will automatically be branded a killer and she will be on the run. Where can you take her and what sort of life will she have?'

Fatema could see his dilemma. The case looked black, in sharp contrast to the evening sky outside where stars danced in the blackness. 'Don't you realise that you are making it look worse this way. How is this helping?' she again pleaded.

Oscar dragged his fingers through his hair and then placed his head, now aching from lack of food, on his arms resting on the steering wheel.

Rita, alone with Fatema and Oscar now, at last accepted Hana's crime but knew that there was much more to be told which would pardon her action. The pressure had been too great. There must be more.

'Oscar, at least let us talk to her.'

'If I do, Fatema, you must not tell anyone if it looks as though we can't help her. I can't let them have her. She's just a kid.'

'Let me talk with my father. Look, I have to be out late so I must tell them something. At the same time, he has experience with the law and he is known in this emirate. Maybe he can act for her or can find someone with a good name to work with her.'

Fatema was talking sense, Oscar knew that but he knew there had not been any sense or reason playing in Hana's life since she came to the house in Ras Al Jebel.

'Where is she?'

'The camel camp… You must swear that you will never talk about it. It is for a special type of training. Your own men are out there, Rita. If you noticed, it is out of this emirate and it is not official. Maybe you could say it is not legal. I can't talk about it but let me tell you, these men care and will help.'

This was a side of Oscar Rita had never seen. What was he talking about? What was this camp? What sort of training was going on?

He would talk no more about it and Fatema was even more convinced that they had to get Hana back into a recognised line or she would end up a rebel or worse, a victim innocent of the blood on her hands. She pressed Oscar firmly and at last her strength won and he slowly shook his head.

'I thought we could smuggle her out of the country. As it is, she is not in this emirate any longer. We wanted to keep her away from the law here. If they catch her outside, they can't arrest her.'

'If she has been led to this, the law should deal justly with her. Don't believe all you hear about our system. Our religion stands for justice too, you know.'

'I know. It's just that she is a foreigner and a woman and it is her word against a dead man's body. How fair do you think they'll be?'

'I think we should see her tonight. How are you explaining your absence from the family you work for? They must be suspicious by now.'

'Don't worry about that. All right, she's out at the camp. I couldn't let you see her until I was sure that this was the best way. I can take you back out there.'

'Why don't you take us all back to the embassy? I can get food and we women can stay with her there tonight. It won't be so far for you to travel and we have the phone on. No one would think of looking there. Anyway, you are going to have to bring her in sometime,' she hesitated, 'or are you going to invite the lawyer and the police out to your camp?'

They weakly smiled at the thought of such a scenario and he started the engine again.

'Maybe it is better if we come with you. The police will be looking for a woman alone and you will be too noticeable if there is a road block. I'll get another *abaya* from home on my way through town. Then I can see my father quickly, get his advice or calm him down if necessary. He'll deal with my mother. She worries more about me.'

Fatema was in charge now and gave a burst of confidence to the other two. 'I'll ring Fereshteh. She'll organise some food – that way people in our house won't know what is going on. The less they know right now the better.'

Ras Al Jebel was a small town, though, and news had travelled throughout the day. The local radio station had reported the death of the old man and the newsreader had announced that Hana was wanted for questioning about the stabbing.

Fatema's father was not surprised when she gave a quick, brief summary of the day's events. 'Do this one legally, madam.' He always addressed her with the polite form. 'I'll do what I can but hiding like this doesn't look good.'

'Well, at least it has given friends some time to think this through. Just a few hours more and perhaps we can strengthen her case...if she has done it, that is.' Fatema still had a doubt and was worried about Oscar's involvement with the camp.

'As soon as you are ready, let me know and I can contact the police for you. It might look better coming from me. I know this family well and this is all a bit delicate. Take care,' and he gave the religious salutation which showed Fatema at once that he was worried.

She was waiting quietly in one of the huts. It was as if she had known they would come. They greeted each other without words. She was silent, frozen in a grief which bore no explanation. Rita held her hand and they wrapped the *shehla* around her head in such a way that it was not obvious who wore it. For once she was glad of this cover.

The journey back to the embassy was tense. It was late now and there was little traffic on the Ras Al Jebel roads. Oscar knew that the police sometimes patrolled, checking stray cars and youths involved in high jinks around the town. He had heard too that any gathering which looked suspicious could be interrupted. How strange was a pick-up truck with an Asian driver and three women, he wondered.

The guards at the gate were surprised to see the truck driving in so late. One of them wandered up to check but Fatema interrupted him.

'It's all right. We've some things to get finished. We're staying late. The driver is going now.'

Oscar frowned, annoyed that the segregation would keep him away from Hana and the women from here on. He was not confident that this was the best move. He wondered about loyalty. Which was stronger – the struggle for right or the ties of culture, of nation maybe. He suspected that with Fatema, there was something else – an energy for women's place in society, a fight for justice in its own way. He trusted her but of this system he was not so sure.

'Thank you,' she spoke loudly. 'Don't worry. Here's my number. We'll be in my office but don't mention this,' she continued softly, holding out her palm on which she had written the direct telephone number.

He memorised it and thought he would remember it all his life.

Fereshteh was waiting at the side entrance, sitting on the steps. Beside her she had several large plastic bags with Choitram's Supermarket written in large green letters. They helped her carry her things inside as she was embracing Hana.

Fatema locked the door behind them, switching off the lights in the passageway as if the darkness would somehow protect them.

Before any questions were asked, Fatema ordered everyone to clean up. The young woman was maternal in her efficiency. Rita and Hana were grateful for the shower. It was as though the skin of depression washed off with the dust and perspiration of the day's journeying. They ate lightly and, though nervous juices had long since quelled their hunger, they felt refreshed with this basic attention to their bodies.

Fereshteh sat quietly in the corner waiting, sketching designs for new wedding celebrations. Fatema sat next to Hana on the couch with Rita at her feet, translating, because the other girl's English had dried up with her vitality.

She told them the whole story, except for the details which she would see over and over in her mind for many months to come.

He had raped her over the week before his death. The last time was the night she had stabbed him. He had not been the only one that night. It was several hours before she again went to his room and killed him. She lapsed into silence. The women could not get her to talk again.

Fatema moved from the couch and asked her to try to sleep while they went to the other room. She covered the girl with a sheet and stroked her head gently. This was not the first time she had dealt with women who had been raped. She had attended a workshop organised by women's crisis centres at the conference in China. She was aware of what to do but knew that the pain was deeper than a sexual penetration, however cruel. A spirit had been broken – much more delicate than the torn flesh. Virginity was not the issue here, though Fatema knew that they would have to make the most of that. It was the woman's soul. Her dignity had been cast out like scraps to the dogs.

'There's a strong case here, surely!' Fereshteh said when Fatema came into the room. 'I felt this would happen months ago. I tried to warn her but they don't have much option here.'

'We have to get her to go to the police. I can go with her. People here know that I went with our national delegation to Beijing. It was in the newspapers and they interviewed me on the radio. I think this will help but we must get her legal representation as well. My father will help.'

'Lucy will want to see her. She has already contacted the embassy and they said they would try to help but they didn't seem sure what they could do at this stage.'

'Did she give you any more details which you haven't translated, Rita?' Fatema asked the other young woman, now quite drawn and tired.

'No, but I'm sure there is much more and I think when she gives her statement to the police, we should be there to make sure that what they write in English or Arabic is exactly what she is saying to us in Tagalog.'

'Yes, I agree. It is likely she won't be able to tell her story very clearly in English after all this and we must find out as much as we can. Someone needs to check her statement to make sure it is accurate. I don't think they will let you, Rita, because you are her friend. Maybe they will bring someone from the embassy or they might allow Lucy, even though she is from the same agency.'

As far as Fatema could see, there was little else they could do that night and they agreed to try to sleep. The next day, all three wanted to be with Hana to help her through the most difficult part. There were many difficult days to come, though, and as time went on, the women found that they could do less and less.

There were many things to be done. The reality of their actions did not penetrate any of them for some time. Even as she signed a statement admitting that she had stabbed the old man, Hana did not fully accept that she was seen as the guilty one, even in her very act of being alive. If she had died, there might have been more sympathy from some quarters.

Oscar was sullen and irritable. He believed he knew their mentality – she was guilty because she had been violated. The death was one more sign of that and he told them so many times over the next few days as he was interviewed officially, and then with less patience by the sons of the family. He told only part of the story.

He had gone back to the house unsuccessfully mimicking an innocent man. He had his own trial by questioning. He had been missing with Hana since they had found the old man's body earlier that morning. It had been half carried, half dragged into the main bedroom at the front of the house. Oscar had known it was useless because the trail of blood from Hana's room would raise more questions than either of them could answer, though somehow he believed removing the body would give them enough time to plan an escape. By the time the family found the body, Hana could be out of the emirate and they could decide the next move.

He had connections. Hana had known that Oscar had friends who believed that overcoming oppression and fighting were one and the same. He had talked to her about it. She was not sure she believed him, though, because she had seen years where fighting had achieved little in Mindanao. She was surprised just the same when he had taken her by the family truck to the camp. She had not been so far from town into the desert except on the roads to Al Shams and Dhahabi. This was different.

As the truck rattled over the rocky ground, she felt light-headed. The reality of what had happened was yet to strike. For now, she had only a sense of relief and release from torment. The rush of adrenalin brought a feeling like excitement. She had no fear at this stage. She had saved herself.

She had looked across at Oscar and forgetting the reason, wondered at his strained face and his silence. There was much about this man she did not know and as they pulled up outside the barbed-wire fence and the iron farm gate which led to the compound of the camp, she wondered if she had ever known him.

Oscar talked with the two men who greeted him; the one with a gun Hana did not recognise. They disappeared for a few minutes and emerged from the hut with another man in jeans and T-shirt. He was older than the others. Like them, he was Asian. They greeted Hana and the leader invited her inside.

'Our friend here has told us what has happened to you, sister. We need to meet with the others to decide if this is the wisest plan.' He looked at the slim woman, doubting whether she could make the trek through the desert even if they agreed to help her escape. 'Have you done much walking, trekking, you know…like soldiers do?'

Slowly Hana realised that she was in a delicate position. She had destroyed the old man's advances in order to keep her own dignity and respect, but now her freedom was in danger whatever happened. She nodded, unsure of what she was accepting. It was many hours later, after listening to the men come and go, listening to their arguments and suggestions and their final decision that overland was not the way to go, that she heard the vehicle pull up with her friends outside.

'Wait, sister. We don't want them to know you are here yet. Once they agree to help you if you go to the police, we will take you to them. If not, it is better that no one knows you are here.'

She had watched them go again and felt very much alone. Some of the men here were Filipinos. They were kind and seemed to understand her predicament. For her part, she would be glad to be free of the house and would accept anything to escape the harsh environment.

In the months to come, Fatema followed the media carefully. She watched the newspapers with more attention than she had ever done. There were many small stories about the ill-treatment of women in service – things which she had read about in literature, things which had been happening decades before in Europe, were happening here and in other newly rich countries throughout the region. The only difference was that now she could see the consequences, the suffering and the rejection. She contacted other women's groups in the country and found there was a lot of support but little organisation. From the beginning she knew good legal representation was crucial and her father had arranged this.

The lawyer was a Palestinian woman. She had worked on human rights cases with Bosnian women. Her name was Layla Ashrawi. She was good in her field but this was a difficult place for a woman lawyer. Layla was there from the beginning. She joined the small group of women in the early hours of the morning and listened to what they related before waking Hana.

'Leave her. She obviously feels safe with you and goodness knows she's going to need all her strength over the next few days. Don't worry about anything else,' she said speaking directly to Fatema. 'Your father has arranged for me to stay up here and I have put off all other cases for several weeks. This is going to take all my attention. It won't be easy.' She outlined the likely progress of events and the interpretation which would be made by the media, the family and various groups supporting each side.

Rita was glad she had written to Hana's family and Alim. They would be sure to hear of this through the media, and they needed to know Hana's story before it was twisted or reduced to bare essentials to be further shot down in print.

They brewed coffee, warmed the leftover food from the evening before and woke Hana. Trying to be cheerful in these circumstances sounded empty and shallow but some of them did it anyway. There was little else they could do now that Hana had agreed to go to the police. She had killed him but it was in self-defence as far as she was concerned. Going to the police seemed a safer option than continually running from them – the alternative Oscar emphasised over and over.

Layla hardly spoke – just a question here and there to encourage the girl, still chilled and distant. She knew the facts but, like Rita and Oscar, was sure there was more. There would be time for that later.

'If you are ready, I'll call the police. It's almost eight and club members will be coming in soon. It is better to go early.'

'Get your father to speak with them too,' Layla advised. 'It should be possible that we can be met by only one or two – not the whole station. Ask him to say she is coming in voluntarily and there should be no shackles,' and with an order rather than request, 'tell him we're both coming with her.'

Rita and Fereshteh hugged the girl once again, intent and outwardly calm. Perhaps she was resigned to her fate, something she had never been before.

She showered – preparation of the victim rather than cleansing of the sinner.

Oscar waited by the gate, offering to drive Fatema's car. This time the three women bundled into the back seat together.

Fatema's father walked through the iron gates, open now to allow cars to move in and out for inspection. With him was an officer, recognisable in his uniform and by his gait. The first man was handsome in his ruggedness but Hana's gaze fell to the ground as she remembered the last group of men to approach her back at her house. The men greeted her in Arabic and the small group continued inside, leaving Oscar by the car.

There were curious eyes all around. Some were waiting for appointments. Others lounged waiting for or avoiding work. There were casual workers and members of the force, all of them men. They lined the veranda built to keep the summer sun off the small, confined offices. Others peered through windows, curious about the young woman who could have been the one in their own house. They had heard the story as were many more to hear it over the following months. Some sniggered – so young. All looked in awe, 'so frail'. She did not look as if she had any more fight in her than a young gazelle.

Fatema held her arm, as much in sympathy as to guide her. The two men led the way into a larger room and the officer dismissed all but two other officers, one male, the other a woman who had come from Dhahabi that morning.

'It is not usual to allow others in while statements are being given,' the officer said, looking at Fatema and her father. 'However, as you have encouraged this young woman to give herself up, we may allow it this time,' he said, knowing that they had no intention of leaving the room.

The phone rang. The woman lifted the receiver and spoke in Arabic.

The translator had arrived. A few seconds later, Lucy walked into the room with another officer who was immediately dismissed. She put her arm around Hana's shoulder and a policeman frowned at her.

'We need the statement in Arabic or English but as the woman does not have fluent English, we shall allow clarification from the translator.'

Layla had insisted on this.

'But remember, you are to translate only what she says and only what we ask. There is to be no elaboration.'

Lucy realised that her own statements would be important because Hana had approached her long before with harassment stories. Why did this have to happen now? It was her first chance to work in the Middle East and already she was embroiled in a court case. As she looked at Hana sitting pensively there in the police station, she felt ashamed. The girl had been raped. There was no doubt of that. She could have wept for the young woman when they asked where she had been in the last twenty-four hours and whether she had been with any men in that time. It was the same in so many places. Women were guilty.

'We have to think this through and not give up. Standing by her solidly and keeping the true story in the public is better than wearing ourselves out fighting petty prejudice,' Layla cautioned. 'Just be sure that what they write is what she told you. There must not be any confusion. It is going to be hard enough as it is.'

For the first time that day, Hana lifted her head and looked at the men. 'I don't want them here when I tell you what happened.'

There was confusion. Fatema's father wanted to help. The police officers knew that they should be present but in the end only the superintendent stayed and the woman from Dhahabi carried out the questioning, taking notes as she did so.

In various ways they all heard Hana's story or parts of it many times over the next few months but none of those tellings had as much impact as the first occasion here in the Ras Al Jebel office where the air conditioning unit almost drowned out the voice, determined and harsh in its nervous shrillness.

# 12

# September–October 1999

*Time: 09.00*
*Date: 30 September 1999*
*Division: Ras Al Jebel*
*Attending Officer: Al Khaiyum*
*Statement issued: Hanan Janjalani*

*'The old man had been coming to me for a long time asking me to come with him and to kiss him and things like that. Nearly two weeks ago things got worse and I felt like people thought I was either making this up or I was being too strict so I kept quiet.*

*'One afternoon when I was in the old man's house preparing food, he came in and asked me to come to his room. He said he wanted to move the table and couldn't lift it by himself. I didn't want to go because every time I was alone with him, he said things to me.'*

'What sort of things did he say to you?'

Hana answered and Lucy translated in full detail, though the officer did not write her responses. Layla also wrote throughout the interview without interjecting but signalled to the officer when she thought Hana needed to rest.

*'We moved the table and he quickly came around to me and asked me why I did not like him. I felt bad because he had not really done anything terrible at that stage. I talked with him and he touched me a little bit.'*

Hana remembered that he had stroked her breast not unpleasantly. For once she was not revolted. Perhaps it was right, she thought. It was just harmless attention that he needed.

He stood closer, running his fingers gently around both breasts, not large but showing themselves through her blouse. 'You know, Hana, there is nothing wrong with men and women showing each other how they feel. Do you like this?'

Hana was confused because she enjoyed his touches but was repulsed at the same time. His hands moved down her body, back to her breast, and she was aware that the sensation was pleasant.

He stood closer and this time she could feel him as he pressed into her. He kissed her throat.

'No, please,' she said and had a strange feeling of nausea and, at the same time, a sensation of need deep down in her.

He sensed it and his hand moved further. She knew for certain now that it was not unpleasant but this was not the way she wanted it. Not with him. Not like this. Face flushed, she pulled away. He looked sad more than anything else and she was not sure how she should respond.

'Just lie with me a minute then,' and he gently pulled her to the bed.

She wanted to stop but was curious at the same time. What would happen?

'Hana, have you been with a man before?'

How often she had been asked this question but never by a man. Her heart thumped and her head pounded as she repeated to herself, 'Move, move.' She rolled away and said she would come back. She ran from the house as she had many times before for the same reason.

The next day she had seen him several times. He looked at her but did not come near, not until that evening. It was late and the houses were quiet.

There was a soft knock on her door and he came in with a box of chocolates. 'Why don't you make us some coffee, Hana.'

'Not here. I'll put it in the dining room.'

He followed her to the stove and when she had filled the pot and picked up a cup, he placed a second one beside it and told her to take it to her room. 'We'll wake the others. There we can chat quietly.'

It seemed a reasonable request but something was warning Hana at the same time as it was enticing her. 'Let's have it here,' she said with some authority now.

He picked up the tray, waiting no longer. She stood at the door of the bedroom, every instinct in her pointing to danger. She was like one of the stray neighbourhood cats now, tempted by the bait of food but wary of the tempter and an undefined danger.

Sitting on the carpet piece, he poured the coffee and beckoned to her to sit beside him. She took the coffee he offered and sipped it once before he took the cup back and drank the rest. She gasped. This went against all that she knew of masters and servants and between this man and herself. The action was very intimate.

She took the other cup and held tight as she finished the liquid. As he opened the box of chocolates, she could not help reflecting on the luxury of the situation – the room, simple, clean and her own, expensive delights, a situation with a hint of romance about it. He offered her a chocolate with his fingers, making her bite it but finishing the rest himself. The syrup trickled from the edge of his mouth and she licked her own lips feeling them sticky.

It was the signal he needed, though she never knew it. He pushed her flat on the floor and smothered her face and neck with his lips still smelling of chocolate. His hands roamed now, everywhere. She could feel his hand on her bare leg, moving upwards. She could no longer stop him. The rough fingers played with the soft hair in a way that she had never done herself and then he stroked her. Involuntarily she moaned but this time could not push away as he was too heavy on top of her.

'Let me, let me! Just touch me,' and he had her hand on his erect penis, hard and warm.

She was surprised and she moved her hand.

'No! Keep it there.'

She was repulsed but fearful of hurting him.

His fingers went into her. It hurt. He groaned loudly and she felt something wet and as sticky as the syrup from the chocolate spill over her fingers. As he slumped beside her, she pulled way, looked at her hand and looked at him.

'Too quickly this time, girl, but next time it will be slower,' he said standing up, rubbing himself with his clothes where she had touched him minutes before. He turned and left, leaving the young woman feeling dirty but still not sure what had happened.

'Why didn't you tell someone?' the officer asked.

'I felt it was my fault and I was frightened I would lose my job,' she answered through Lucy.

'I could not lock my door so I pulled the bed up against it. Then he could not come in again but the next night he did not come or if he did I did not hear him try the door. I felt safe.

'I did not see him during the next day. I think he went out. Sometimes he used to go to his camel farm, although it has been too hot to be outside. Perhaps he went to see them. That night I knew some of the people in our house were going to visit the other family. I thought I should get to bed early as I did not have to prepare a meal. I carried my own food into my room, put the tray on the floor and started to push the bed against the door. I felt someone was in the room and when I turned around he was sitting on the floor in the corner watching.'

Again Hana did not repeat in detail what happened that night. She could not. She was shaking and felt faint. She could not weep now, just as she could not cry out when the old man stood up and pulled her to him again. This time there was no time for talking. He had her lips and his tongue was in her mouth. His hands were all over her, searching, caressing, beating her struggling arms away. Pulling her to the floor, he ignored her protesting, tore her blouse, hungrily though not hurting her, not yet. He lifted her skirt. He knew what he wanted and she suffered pain such as she had never known before but aware now that he was destroying her.

After it was over he turned and said, 'You're mine now, my little bride. I've made you a woman.'

'Hana, are you all right? Could we have some tea, please.' Layla asked, knowing that the shock had been building up too long in the young woman she was going to defend. 'I think we should wait a while before we continue.'

'We should finish the statement today, although she has admitted verbally to stabbing him.'

They all left the room now and left Lucy with her young ward. Lucy had known her for almost a year and could never have seen this in Hana.

Hana sipped her tea and said that she wanted to finish. The others should come back. She could tell them what else had happened.

*'I don't know why but I didn't tell anyone what had happened. I couldn't sleep that night. I kept washing myself but I felt unclean. The next day I told my boss's wife that I felt sick when she said I looked terrible. It was the same thing again. He didn't come near me again and that night I slept but kept seeing him in my dreams. I felt it was my fault – that I had encouraged him. When Oscar spoke to me I was really unkind to him and told him to leave me alone. I didn't mean it. I didn't know what I was doing.*

*'The next night I waited and waited before I went to my room. I kept finding things to do. I kept talking to the women. Maybe they wondered why I was so friendly. I looked for Oscar but he had gone out too. Then as I was walking through the back garden to get back into my room, he stepped out of the garage.'*

'Have you come to find me, Hana? I've been waiting for you.'

'If you touch me, I'll scream. I don't want it. I mean it, I don't want it.'

'Come on,' he laughed softly, believing he knew the girl. He pulled her to the garage, dragged the door down noisily and locked it firmly.

Hana felt sick. She ran to the other door but he came for her, knowing her, she felt, and that made it worse – a mouse teased by a cat who knew it had won.

His lair was the car, a luxury vehicle by any standards.

'Some men dream about this, Hana. I want to make love to you in here,' and he locked the door behind her.

The thing that astounded her most about this was the strength he had for such an old person. She thought it was possible that he was smarter than she was because she could not predict his moves. At that moment she could not escape from the small prison he made for her, a vehicle which many others would have been grateful just to enter.

He forced her several times in that car, somehow stimulated by the strangeness of it all. When he finally let her go, she was exhausted, in pain and a creature beaten beyond recognition. He had finally broken her spirit.

She stared blankly to the window opposite, seeing nothing but what had happened that night. After a long pause, the officer called her name. Looking up with a start, she seemed surprised to see the three woman watching her – two who understood and another who had heard it before.

'What happened after this?' the woman in uniform asked her.

*'He told me to hurry to my room and to close the door after me. I sat there for a long time I think. I can't remember how long but when I left the garage, it was almost light. I could hear the prayers from the mosque.*

*'I didn't go into the house again. I walked out of the front gate because I wanted to find Rita. I couldn't think what to do.'*

In a daze, she walked to the corner where the wide, gravelled road met the asphalt road, broken along the edges from where the winter rains had torn it away. She started to walk, one foot in front of the other, energy slowly rising within her. Walking gave her a sense of power. She was now in control. She knew where she was going, though not what she would do once she reached her friends' house.

She did not notice the early-morning workers. From so many countries near her own, they looked at her curiously. It was strange to see a woman, any woman, out so early, walking alone through the dust. The air was already warm and she knew she was thirsty but it no longer concerned her.

With every step she muttered, 'No more, not again, never again.'

She knew she could not go back to the house but could not think beyond the present.

A truck passed. The horn sounded loudly and men called out. She heard nothing. The sound in her brain was his voice and her cries as he pushed into her, over and over again.

Why he would not stop she did not know. He had kept the door shut, determined that she would serve him. The more she pleaded and resisted, the more forceful he became.

He held her head and pushed her down. 'You'll do it!' he ordered, but she did not understand. He instructed, coaxing at first. Then he commanded, 'This is what you should do to make me pleased. That's what you're here for, aren't you, to make me satisfied.'

Goats bleating as another truck swerved to miss them brought her out of her reverie.

'Where are you going?' the driver called from an empty taxi, returning to his rank or perhaps after taking a late-night carouser home.

She ignored him. She trusted no one at that moment.

The vehicle stopped further along the road and the driver, a Filipino like herself, came out to greet her. He asked if everything was all right or if she wanted a lift.

She ignored the first question and responded to the second, giving Rita's street address. The growing realisation of what had happened overcame any caution she might have had before. 'Just leave me here. It's too early to wake them.'

'Look, if I can do anything to help, please let me know. It's not easy here but I know people if you need anything,' he said softly and with concern in his voice.

She nodded, still not looking at him.

In this part of town there was more movement. Many of these people had jobs and their own work to finish before they started on someone else's business.

A jogger passed her. 'Hello, Hana! What are you doing out so early?' It was Rita's employer, running before the air was too hot.

She muttered some response and walked briskly to the front gate, which stood ajar. It was easier visiting here because Rita had her own quarters – a garden shed converted to her own flat. She used the bathroom at the back of the house but lived separately from the family, giving her a feeling of independence, unusual for many of her group.

*'By the time Rita opened her door I was crying so she knew something terrible had happened. She knew anyway because I had never been there so early. She made me coffee.'*

She remembered the jar of instant coffee, which was almost empty. She saw the flask, which had hot water from the night before, water still warm enough to drink and which refreshed her after her walk and the night that had gone before it.

*'After a while I told her what had happened and I explained some things of the last few days. She told me I could stay with her whatever happened. Then she said she would have to say something to her boss so she went into the house. I don't know what she said but she told me I could stay there for a while.'*

Layla knew that Rita did not have all the details. There were things Hana was saying that she had not heard before. She would interview this woman many times over the next few weeks to make sure she knew all that had happened, all that was threatened and all that was suggested during those weeks and months in the dead man's house.

*'I think I stayed two days with her. I slept for a long time even though I had been drinking coffee. I showered in Rita's bathroom in the house. It was still quiet. The children were asleep but our friend, the Pakistani lady,*

*came out and asked me what was wrong. I couldn't talk to her. Perhaps she was worried they would be in trouble because she kept asking questions for a while and then left us alone. Then she called Rita and she gave her some puri she had made. I thought she was very kind to do this because Rita was the one who should be cooking for her. This is why I call her our friend. She has always been good to us.*

*'I slept a long time. When I woke up, Rita was not there and I could not think where I was for a minute. Then I felt strange. I ran out to the garden and threw up. In the end I couldn't be sick any more but I kept making the same noise and still felt as if I wanted to be.*

*'They let me stay there all day and when I said I would not go back to that house, Rita let me stay with her. I wanted to stay forever. I did not want to leave her room. I felt like it was my fault but I felt safe. I knew nothing would happen to me there.*

*'Because the children were there, they asked us not to talk about any problems. I helped Rita for a while in the kitchen and then went back to sleep because I could hardly stand up. I had never felt so tired before.*

The women looked up as the air conditioner sighed and stopped.

'Oh no, the power has gone again.'

'There is no generator here so we don't know how long this will last. We must continue because I have to get this full statement today,' the officer said, resigned to the limitations of modern technology in this isolated part of the desert.

She drew the shuttered curtains across the windows, closed against the heat of the sun, high and hot at this time of the year.

Another man in uniform entered, joined by an old man carrying a tray with tea and glasses of water. The officer spoke quickly in Arabic to the woman who was the same rank as he was. The other one looked curiously at Hana. Lucy saw it. Could it have been admiration she detected?

'They have asked if we want to continue under the trees at the back of the building. It is shady there and they will move everyone aside.'

Hana shook her head and the other women were disappointed

because already the room was hot. She had had enough of people, of men, looking at her. She felt exposed and vulnerable. At least here the walls gave her some privacy, though she could not guess what the women before her really thought.

The tape recorder stood idle now. Statements by hand were tedious but the officer listened carefully to the translation as there were other circumstances in this case which could help release this girl.

'That afternoon I sat with Rita outside. We were sorting through the dhal, taking out the stones. The men came around through the side gate. There were three of them...the man who did some cooking at the son's house, and two other men, one I had seen at the old man's house before. They said that my employer had sent them to tell me to come back to my work. I didn't like them at that moment and I did not want to go back to that house. I told them I didn't want to go and Rita said I could stay with her. They said I had to go back because I would be illegal. My passport was with the family and I was on a contract to them. Then they went to the front of the house, I suppose to tell the Pakistani family something because soon they all came back together.

'I think my friends knew it was wrong to send me back but when they called me inside, they told me that I had no choice because my passport was with them and at least I had to go back to ask for it. Rita said she would come with me and they agreed but it didn't help because the men refused to have her in the car.

'I felt shame because I had to get into the car with all those men. It seemed like everyone was watching me. Rita's boss spoke to the other Pakistani man but I didn't trust him. Maybe they didn't either.

'As we were driving back to the house, they kept asking me questions but I didn't answer. I wished I could die right then. When we arrived at my house, I couldn't see anyone but I felt there were people watching from the windows. We all got out together and they told me to go around the back of the house. The old man's son was there. He was very angry and asked where I had been and complained for a long time about how lazy I was, going away with my friends and not doing my work. He said I would lose some salary and that he would contact the agency if I did this again. I wished he would.

'Then he told me I was to stay in the house and look after his father because the wife had gone away for a few days to visit her daughter. I begged him to let me work in his house, with his family, but he ignored me. I don't know if he guessed anything but he would not listen. This was the end. I knew it then. It would not stop and I could not live like this.

The next few hours flashed by her like a recurring nightmare. She saw the details vividly, over and over. He came to her and forced himself again furiously. He had held his hand over her mouth.

When he had gone, a man came. He looked at her – a thrashed, weeping girl, cowering in the corner. Something held him back – perhaps only that he was a worker who could not afford to lose his job.

The walls closed around her and a weight pressed down on her head. There was a silence like a tomb – a void rather than stillness. Swirling red, and then blackness swamped her.

Slowly she recalled why she was on the floor, why she was in pain and what they had done to her. She lay there shivering, a beaten animal.

*He will use me. I have to stop him somehow.* Warnings crashed through her mind in waves, one after the other.

Her eyes rested on the windowsill. She had a few decorative pieces there – a small Chinese vase with some dyed grasses in it, postcards of Quiapo and a glass dish which Asma's daughter had given her at the time of her wedding. The stones lay in it. She could see them through the cut glass and remembered her fury at the man on the Corniche.

Something within her sparked then fumed. She knew then what she would do. She blazed with white-hot fury. In spite of the pain, she sat bolt upright. *He wouldn't touch her again. No one would.*

She saw the leer and the discoloured teeth. Her own were like that now, the thought flashed through her. It was the water – it turned everyone's teeth brown – but that no longer mattered. In a daze, with only one thing before her eyes, she walked slowly to the kitchen.

It had not been clear what she would do until she saw a weapon lying on the marble sideboard. It was large and heavy – a knife they used it for slicing the carcasses of sheep whenever celebrations were held. Perhaps the last time she had washed it was at the wedding.

The touching – he started it this day as on other days but today would be the last time.

She picked up the tool, took the flask of hot water she had earlier prepared for their tea and went back to her room. She placed them carefully on the table she had made from a discarded packing case. As she did, her eyes flicked to the stones which beckoned her to the window. She stepped across and touched them up, rubbing them between her fingers. Some hidden strength seemed to flow from them into her limbs and as the blood poured into her face, an energy and calm welled up in her. If she had to stay here, she would do it with some dignity.

*'So when he came back later that night and started to talk, I moved to my table because the knife was under my scarf which I had thrown on top of it. He started saying things again. He said he wanted to be my friend, that I was beautiful and all of this. I told him to go away but he took no notice. He pulled me again and pushed me onto to bed. He was old but he was strong. This time I didn't try to scream because I couldn't get away. When he finished and lay back on the pillows, I leant over to the table and took the knife.*

She looked at each of the women.

*'I pushed it into him. I wanted to stop him hurting me ever again. He did the bad things to me but somehow he made me feel the bad one. I wanted to kill him.'*

She said it simply, emotion spent now. She had stabbed him many times, over and over. Every thrust she gave him seemed to be for those he had forced onto her.

*'I wanted to stop him for all time.'*

There was silence in the room. Though the air was hot and the women were perspiring, they shivered. A cold like marble had touched them.

# 13

# October 1999

Writing was the only thing Rita could do which made her feel useful. It made her feel as though she was doing something to help. Hana had been in the town but not with them for nearly two months. She could just as easily have been a century away. Her friends had no power in this situation but Rita was part of the network, alerting them to the latest movements, expressing her frustration and pleading for some help in this lonely desert town. People had to be aware.

*Post Office Box 20*
  *Ras Al Jebel*
  *15 October 1999*
  *Dear Alim*
    *You must have received my first letter by now. Hana's parents have telephoned the embassy. They want to come over here to see her. The next hearing is in two weeks' time. After that is over there should be a new verdict – at least we are praying so. People say it will also be in a sharia court but there will be a new judge. You might know what that means, although things are different from this at home.*
    *I have not been allowed to visit Hana. No one has except Layla and the other lawyer who is helping her. I think someone from the embassy has been but I can't go until after the court's business is over. She has been moved to the women's prison in Al Shams because there are no other women here and they say it is not proper for her to be kept alone. Layla says not to worry. She tells us that Hana looks all right – just pale. She is very quiet and her eyes*

*seem tired. Maybe she is not eating much. She says they treat her properly but she can't sleep.*

*I have heard this new prison is clean. From the outside it looks better than some of our government buildings in Manila. Layla is says it is like other prisons but not as bad as those in her land.*

*I didn't know this before but there are other Filipina women there but I don't know what they have done. This makes me really sad. We are not told these things when we apply for work in these countries. I really want to come back home but please don't worry. I won't go until this business with Hana is sorted out.*

*Last time Layla visited, I begged her to let me go with her but I could only go as far as the gate. I could see a gold minaret in the grounds. There is a small mosque there. Layla told me that many of the workers and officers are women. It is difficult to know how the women are treated but I hope that because Hana's case has been in the newspapers so much, that nothing bad happens to her in prison.*

*Let me tell you what has happened because my last letter was short and there was so much to say.*

*Some day I will tell you how we went with Hana to the police station in Ras Al Jebel. That was a day and night I shall never forget. I hope we have done the right thing. Some friends wanted to try to get her out of the country but it is difficult where we are and we probably would not have been able to get her home in any case and then what would happen?*

*They held the first hearing fairly quickly. There were many questions asked by everyone. The family was terribly angry and they wanted Hana to pay with her life. We were not allowed to the court so I am telling you what I have read in the newspaper and what our friends Fatema and Layla told us.*

*There was a lot of talk in the court and both sides told stories a bit different from each other about what had happened. They both agreed that Hana had stabbed the old man because she admitted it, so Layla tried to get the judge to understand that she had been treated in a very bad way by the old man. Of course, Layla had to work through another lawyer but she was convinced that he was representing Hana as well as she could.*

*At the end of the first hearing, the judge sentenced Hana to seven years'*
*imprisonment for killing the man. We were shocked. It was so unjust!*
*Hana had been tormented. She was not guilty of murder. It was more like*
*self-defence. We think they wanted to teach us all a lesson.*

*Alim, you won't believe it, the family also objected but for a different*
*reason from us. They are saying the sentence is too light for the death of*
*their father and grandfather. I think maybe they have been higher up.*
*Others think that those higher up or those in the embassy or somewhere*
*might know the sentence is too harsh but they can't just say it, especially*
*because the family is so angry. That's why they are having a new trial and*
*hopefully, a new verdict.*

*I am sorry this letter is so sad but we are hoping for better news. Please*
*write to Hana if you can. Don't be ashamed. It is different here and we*
*feel on our own. Thank goodness we have people like Fatema and Layla*
*to support us. It is difficult for me in my work because the family I work*
*for know that I am Hana's friend and everyone is talking about what has*
*happened. She is my friend, though, and I will be her friend till the end*
*of my life.*

*Please give my good wishes to your family. I only met them a couple of*
*times but maybe they remember me. I think some people will help Hana's*
*parents with the air fare.*

*Your friend*

*Rita*

Rita wrote several times to Alim over the next few weeks but it was
the last desperate telegram which raised a brief phone call to Rita's
workplace.

'Rita, there is a person-to-person phone call for you from the
Philippines.'

She ran to the phone in the kitchen. She rarely received calls at the
house but her employers knew what was happening with Hana's case.
It was the talk of Ras Al Jebel and of many of the small emirates and
countries in the region.

The next verdict shocked them all. No one anticipated this turn of events and the whole Filipino community in the emirates was shattered. Many in the Arab community were also surprised but Fatema, Layla and those involved intimately with the case would not accept this decision. They were determined to fight.

'Hello? This is Rita.'

'Rita, it's Alim. By God, is this true that they want to kill her? Can't you do something?'

'Oh, Alim, thank goodness you rang. Yes, they say it was premeditated murder because Hana stabbed this old –' she used a Maguindanao word that men often shouted as the lowest term of abuse '– more than thirty times. I don't see what difference it makes and it just shows how terrified she was of what had happened to her.'

'What is the embassy doing there? The story is in all the papers here and everyone is up in arms. Some groups are talking about what really happens to our people working in other countries. Some of the unions are getting support from unions in other countries but what can I do?'

'Look, Alim, I'll write as soon as I can find out what will happen now. The judge said that there could be an appeal in fifteen days. I'll write when...'

The line went dead. Rita knew how much money the young driver had spent making that phone call. She could picture it now. Maybe the people of Quiapo had collected enough for Alim to call. They were probably standing around waiting for his news of the young girl they had seen so happy in their area a year before. She could hear them – angry, disbelieving, wanting to fight – but what could they do from there?

News spread quickly through their community. The ambassador was appealing through recognised legal channels but had assured them that he would approach the rulers themselves if this did not lead to reconsideration. Other friends had told her that they had heard that their president in Manila was going to appeal personally at the highest diplomatic level. On a different plane, Filipino workers were less hopeful. A different kind of justice was in place here. It was *diya*. The old man's family were aggrieved and therefore in a powerful position.

'But how can they do this? Everyone must be able to see she is just a girl...a good girl, an innocent girl!' Oscar had expected the worst. He had been in the region long enough to understand that their way of seeing things was not the same as his, particularly when women were involved. 'She's a foreigner but at least I thought they might take into consideration that her religion is theirs. What can you expect? We are just cheap labour for them!' He could not come to terms with the decision and stormed away from the van which had brought the Iranian and Filipino women to meet Fatema.

Fereshteh understood what had happened and tried to calm the angry Filipinas, crying in frustration. Fatema looked on wondering how long it would take them to realise the difficulty of her position. She had dedicated herself to her women but the answer always remained that their way was different and that she could not change their culture. She thought differently, however, and so did some others like her father and those like Layla and Fereshteh.

'They can't kill her. Oh God, this could happen to any of us. We've all heard these stories and how can we escape? Now we are powerless. We have no passport and no money. Who can help Hana? Her family is like mine, only poorer. How can they do this?'

Fatema had explained the family's right for *qasas*. Under sharia law, they could demand a death sentence since Hana's killing determined her own death. She had warned them that the youngest son had resorted to this traditional plea in the first week of the appeal hearing but Rita had hoped that fairness would win.

Like Hana, Rita was really a village girl in her ways. They had been brought up in an environment which was warm and forgiving though strict. For Rita, forgiveness was everything. Catholics were lucky that way, she used to say to Hana. 'We can confess our sins to God by telling the priest and he will forgive us,' but then Rita had never known a situation like this before. She knew of the political fighting in Mindanao but that was different from this and she had never been directly involved. She knew *macho* behaviour from her brothers but sexual violence was taboo for them.

Oscar was distraught. He spent more and more time with friends in tea houses at night. Whenever he could find a vehicle free for a few hours, he would go back out to the camp, but employers were wary now and the expatriate Asian workers knew that it was not wise to be seen congregating around town.

Rita had asked him to take her back to the camel camp on her day off. He was not happy with this as anything seemed likely now and the men there had warned him to be careful about raising suspicions. They had only loose connections to the region and as such could also be deported at best, and at worst – they knew too well.

'Look, if I take you out there you have to be absolutely careful not to mention it to anyone. Otherwise that will be the end of all of us and then none of us can help Hana.'

Rita agreed enthusiastically.

They drove out in dull silence until Rita spluttered, 'Why can't we kidnap her? You men have some weapons, at least the guard has. Why don't we find out where they will take her and ambush them?'

'Shut up! Do you want to get us all thrown into jail! You've seen nothing. Understand? Nothing!'

The truth was that Oscar too was so desperate now that he had wondered the same thing but he could no longer think clearly with so little sleep and such feelings of desperation.

They both brought up the subject again when they sat drinking tea with the men at the huts. It was the hottest time of the year and there was no cooling out here, not even an evening breeze, but they sat outside now that the sun had gone down, feeling freer than in the cramped cabins which smelt of food and sweating bodies.

'We could get a false passport but it will take a little time. The quickest way would be to get her on a dhow to India but she'll again face immigration problems unless we can smuggle her all the way. It'd be dangerous but no worse than what faces her at the moment,' said the man Rita recognised from an earlier meeting.

'Our biggest problem is getting her out. If she had still been in Ras Al Jebel it would not have been so difficult but the prison in Al Shams is top security. I don't see how we can do it using ordinary tactics.'

He emphasised the word 'ordinary' and Rita wondered what other tactics he had in mind.

An older man spoke. 'Look here, wait a bit. There is still the chance that they might change the decision.'

Several of the men snorted at him.

'Right! You realise that if we use the tactics you are suggesting, it will mean an end to our training here. Everyone will be after us.'

'So what do you suggest? Leave her to die?' Oscar said with a clenched jaw. 'I'm only saying that we are out here for a purpose and we should plan strategically in this case as well. Let's see what the next two weeks brings.' He turned to Rita. 'What are you friends and the lawyer doing?'

Rita was surprised how much they all seemed to know about the little band of women struggling for Hana. She explained briefly and mentioned the petitioning from Fatema's father and the lobbying of women's groups by Fatema herself.

'OK. That's important because it means there are local people working on her behalf. Unless something else happens to change things, we meet here in two weeks' time to see if there are any results from appeals.' He got up and went into the furthest cabin.

With a rapid jerk, Rita slid her feet to one side, slapped her ankle and rubbed it hard where a desert ant had bitten it.

Oscar touched the coffee pot sitting on the smoldering embers in front of them. He pulled his hand back from the heat and used the flap of his shirt to pick up the metal handle. He filled several mugs silently and then lit a cigarette. He offered one to Rita although he knew she did not smoke.

She shook her head and then asked, 'What do you do out here?'

There was no answer and she knew that, fortunate to have their support, she had now entered forbidden territory. She should have known from home. This was men's business. Even in Mindanao, there were certain roles and information which the men kept to themselves.

'She's all right. I've told her not to talk about us,' Oscar said.

This was the last question Rita asked about the camp but she thought about it for years, even after she had left the Middle East.

The media highlighted the story. Every day, the newspapers reported it – the same bare facts, that she said she had been raped and that she had killed the man. They debated ages. Some said she was sixteen. The family argued that it was a lie, that her papers said she was twenty-seven. Tampering with details on birth certificates and passports so that young people could work became a public issue. Then while the family said their father was in his eighties, others said the old man was thirty years younger than that but the ages remained only one part of this often-repeated story.

There was even a television interview on the BBC, though only Fatema and Layla had seen it, where a women from the Joint Houseworkers Union in Britain had spoken emotionally about what had happened to Hana. Vehemently, she told of workers being caught in webs of indenture and near slavery, where conditions and salaries were so poor that they could not escape. She called on workers to unite against the abuses afflicting these women and men, and called for legal support and diplomatic action to save Hana.

Closer to Hana, her embassy was quieter, not confronting the government, the courts or the family. A deliberate tactic of mediation was in sharp contrast to the alternatives argued for by Oscar and some of his friends. Those who were used to local traditions knew that no one would win if people, proud and defensive of their 'own ways', were pushed into a corner and threatened. They would resist.

Withdrawn from the negotiating around her, Hana sank lower, dreaming sometimes. There were sometimes happy dreams though frequently the nightmares played before her like a movie set while she waited to be swamped again.

Once, she woke up sobbing. She had dreamt of coconut palms, huge banana leaves swaying in the breeze, and creeping vines calming and soothing her. Then the vines grew and grew, and swirled in front of her, around her, between her legs and around her throat. They caught her, wrapped her up and malevolence engulfed her. As she suffocated, she tried to scream but the vines around her throat wound tighter and tighter. There was no one to help.

# 14

# October–November 1999

*you fly free my friend*
*across the sands*
*who knows what you have seen*
*have you heard the tears shaken on the earth*
*tears of others like me*
*a poor bird captive*
*lost*
*calling out to be saved*
*you fly free my friend*
*across the rivers*
*and oceans*
*have you seen people locked and bound*
*some for no sin but their poverty*
*weak*
*because they are the forgotten ones*
*you fly free my friend*
*go across the ocean for me*
*take me with you*
*can you hear me calling you*
*your brothers and sisters know my sin*
*I did it*
*to be free*

*HJ 1999 Al Shams*

The sounds were what Hana would remember most clearly all her life. For much of the time, she remained in a daze. She obeyed orders – the voices, the public address system, the bells and alarms. She had always been obedient.

*Why didn't I stay at home and marry when my father told me?* She knew what had happened but knew that she had had no alternative. She felt trapped whatever happened.

She went to prayers but her heart was elsewhere – surrounded by greenery, swaying palms, lapping waves and laughing red lips but not prayer mats, marble and concrete courtyards. She went through the motions – washing, standing, kneeling and bowing low. Her lips moved but her words were more of supplication than praise – *save me, save me.*

Layla became her strongest support. The guards were not unkind when they called her to the interview room when her legal advisor came but their job would not allow sympathy to affect their treatment of prisoners.

When she was not working, she would sit staring into the courtyard. Pigeons fluttered there if it was quiet. They became her friends she believed, and she listened for them each morning and afternoon as the sun rose and set. With no possessions in her cell, they became the finest gift of her life but she told no one for then they could not be taken from her.

'Hana, they will try for another verdict soon. They are looking at the evidence again but more importantly they are talking with the family. In this country and in this court, what they want is very important.'

Hana sighed but did not answer.

'Your parents are coming.'

The young woman's face changed – puzzlement and a relief which let tears flow. 'How can they?' she gasped.

'A lot of people know about you and there is a businessman in your country who has helped them.' Layla talked to her gently of her family and pieced together a picture of her life in Mindanao. 'Be strong. Don't give up. I have seen more hopeless situations and they have worked out. It will take time but be patient.'

Hana had always been seen as a patient, accepting person but here there was a sense of hopelessness because she was seen as a criminal rather than the victim she knew she was.

She heard the bolt slide across and the door swing open but she kept her eyes on the table in front of her. Layla squeezed her hand and was gone.

'Come on, don't be slow,' the voice said and she shuffled back to her room.

In the distance she could hear pans being washed and stacked in the kitchen. Soon it would be her turn but today she was alone again.

Her crime seemed great to some, so she had plenty of hours alone. There were other women from her country. She felt for them, perhaps victims in their own way – for sure victims in their own way. If ever she was free of this, she would work for the poor – never for the wealthy again. *What am I thinking? Free of this? I have been a captive since I arrived – just as much as here.*

Selected visitors came – good women, often religious. They meant well and felt for her in their own way but Hana could not hear their words. Her pigeons gave her more comfort. She saw them as her messengers and dreamed of training one or two who would carry her notes across the sands and above the seas to friends and home, where she belonged. They did not come, of course, but she escaped for a time each day when these birds, her friends, would be her rescuers.

Through it all, her greatest relief became her writing.

*they take us in war*
*yet we join them in the struggle*
*they make us their whores*
*yet we join them as wives*
*they praise us in shrines*
*yet we work on the ground*
*we work at life*

*we work for peace*
*we work in factories*
*we work as servants*
*we fight for justice*
*yet they show us none of it*

*HJ 1999 Al Shams*

In the weeks that went by, there was other writing and negotiation generated by Hana's case. Layla wrote and discussed Hana's case. Officials wrote to other officials, embassy and foreign affairs officers spoke with the ruler's office. Journalists in many countries wrote and rewrote stories about the young prisoner and photos of a waif-like woman-child caught the attention of readers who heard more and more stories about abused workers from poor Asian countries.

Rita wrote letters – many of them – to Hana, Alim and her own parents and sisters who were just as worried about her. In desperation she even contacted the Catholic priest in Dhahabi. In her own country many of these men were prepared to risk their own lives for the poor and abused, and who, she wondered, could be poorer in spirit than Hana. They spoke to the embassy officials but could do little more than offer advice which was already being given. Rita felt let down. She could not allow herself to think about what would happen if Hana did not gain a reprieve.

Then it happened.

'Rita, Oscar is asking for you at the side gate. Maybe he has more news.'

Her employers had supported her as much as they dared in this small town. They knew that Hana had been tormented but also knew that speaking out publicly about this case would do them no good. They needed the work here and knew that work permits were renewed on the basis of recommendations or rejected if there was personal criticism or recrimination.

She knew immediately from Oscar's face that something had happened.

'Quick! Fatema called. She's at the embassy and wants us to meet her there. I have to collect Fereshteh on the way.'

The message was simple: *Reduced sentence other conditions letter following Lily.*

A letter was posted the same day, along with another to her sister in Mindanao.

*22 November 1999*

*Dear Alim*

*Well, I don't know whether to be glad or sad. Our lawyer friend rang us at the embassy today and gave us the verdict of the appeal's court. I don't know how things work in this culture but perhaps you will understand this better than I do.*

*First it was seven years in prison, then it was the death sentence and now – it is one year in jail, one hundred lashes and money.*

*I can't bear this any more. I want to leave this country. That man raped her again and again and now they will lash her. I'm sorry to upset you but where is the justice? Fatema's father says that they won't hurt her. It is only meant to shame her. Why shame her? It is the man who should be shamed.*

*I suppose you understand this payment thing. They are calling it 'diya' in Arabic. It's like blood money. It is more money than we could all earn in one lifetime together. It is one hundred and fifty thousand dirhams, which is about one million two hundred thousand pesos!*

*The money is out of the question for her family but there is no problem about that because Lucy said either the embassy will pay it or there are business people in this country and in the Philippines who are sorry about Hana's life here. Nobody could help that. There have been many photos in the newspaper and I cry whenever I see her. We're young and we haven't done anything bad in our lives for this sort of thing to happen. She's not the only one, you know. This sort of thing is going on with lots of others.*

*Next thing, Alim – Layla said Hana received your card. Please write to her again. She has to remember how we all love her and do not feel ashamed of her. I feel proud of what she did but if I say that I'll lose my job and right now all I want to do is pay my debts, wait for Hana and come back to the Philippines when she does in one year's time. They will deport her as soon as she gets out of jail. She needs us and we all need you and other friends.*

*It is good that her parents came. I spoke to them last week in Al Shams. Maybe you met them when they were in Manila. I am so sad for them. Her mother reminds me of my own mother. They have never travelled before and think about how bad this is for them. Everyone has been so helpful. Filipino businessmen here raised money for their trip and the embassy people have tried so hard for Hana.*

*Please give my best wishes to your family.*

*Your friend*

*Rita*


The decision was still not seen as a just one by many. For several days, newspapers wrote as though the family had been generous, reconciling themselves to the family of the woman who had killed their father. There were photos of the two families meeting on the steps of the court and of Hana's smiling father handing over a cheque to the old man's sons. Many were incensed with the reporting but those who knew the ways of this country and its people understood that this was a face-saving act. At no stage was the memory of the old man to be reviled or his person rebuked in the press. The most that could be written, and it continued to be written nine months later when Hana was released and deported, was that he had allegedly raped the girl.

The families were silent. The embassy was non-committal and although this decision was denounced in many countries, there was no public outcry in the Gulf, as people thought it was the lesser of the many evils which could be laid upon the young woman.

Oscar and Rita could not accept the thought of one hundred lashes. No matter what Fatema advised, they were disturbed enough to renew efforts to release her. Reports of the lashing, which was to take place in two sessions over the month of December, created an outcry in the foreign press and media, though none of it was reported in the Gulf papers. An Australian woman showed Lucy an article from a Melbourne newspaper. It was only one of many which had appeared in the Western press, she said – cold hard facts presenting a harsh reality, swept aside in public like the blinding sands of desert storms. They both knew that this type of reporting, from vantage points so different from these ancient desert societies, could not capture the nuances of the situation.

For some, the prison sentence would be accepted. In other countries the plea would be different. The *diya* could also be accepted as a cultural peculiarity, but the lashing was seen as the rape repeated again and again. This woman had known humiliation and pain from the man's thrusting and force.

What the public never knew was that there was more than one man involved in Hana's torture. Another walked freely in the streets, for Hana refused to make his crime public, fearing more publicity and attention.

'Look, this is no consolation but have you noticed how often there are reports in our newspapers over the last few weeks about the treatment of workers and housemaids particularly, in this area and in other Asian countries,' Fatema interjected when Rita and Lucy were arguing about Hana's threatened punishment.

'So that makes it all right? She's the sacrificial lamb! We don't believe in that any more.'

'Calm down, Rita. She has a point and anyway Fatema doesn't agree with this any more than we do. Her father has tried in his own way but what can be done? Fatema –' she turned to the woman who had publicised this story through her own networks '– do you think Layla will be able to get us to see Hana?'

'Now that's another thing! My father is using all his connections to help us do that but you have to remember that Hana might not be as happy to see us as we would think. Remember that she was trying to tell you two that this was going on.'

The silence was broken only by the prayer call from the neighbourhood mosque nearby.

'I've also decided to leave here when Hana is released and if I can't get immediate release, I'll go at the end of the next year. I have already spoken to the agency and to our embassy officials. If you are serious about leaving too, Rita, you have to do something about it. We're not free to just go whenever we want.'

'Perhaps you could do more good here, consulting with the women you bring over to work. People are talking about the age thing and changing the documents but that is still not going to solve problems of abuse,' Fatema said guardedly.

Lucy shook her head. 'We're all part of this, each one of us, but I'm not the one to solve the problem here. Let me know if we can visit Hana. I have to go back to Dhahabi.' She looked at Rita as she walked to the door. 'The only person who can help Hana now is you, Rita. You are her friend and her sister.'

# 15

# December 1999

The grating hum of the cicadas disturbs her reverie. There are many sounds but she focuses on a few of them – the sounds which have become her closest companions over the past months. She has spent much time alone but knows of the others. They have become part of her ambition, her vocation – for now she has a special calling that she will never forget.

'If all others forget you, I shall never forget you,' Rita had written as had another, thousands of years before.

A year has passed and in that, she has become a woman but without dignity. She has known love and lust and rape. She knows death but is like rock in her determination to overcome force and violence. She understands struggle now and will join others, though for the present they will see no emotion on her face. There are others, she tells herself over and over.

She writes. Her plans and consolation rest in that alone.

*24th December 1999*

*Al Shams*

*I shall never forget this day because this evening I hear I am to be beaten. I am afraid, though I have been beaten before in a worse way in this land. I feel sick at heart and I am angry but I hope I don't cry. They should not have that to report.*

*I have been in this country for more than a year. I have had a birthday and have lived in three towns and I feel as if it has been for three lifetimes.*

*I can only count the time I have left now. Maybe I can leave in seven*

*or eight months. Deportation has never been such a wonderful dream for
a worker here.*

*It is strange that I was weak and ignorant when I came here but now I
have found a strength and know things, see things more clearly.*

*I think of those stones.*

She remembers her anger and humiliation that morning on
the Corniche in Ras Al Jebel, that town which hurt her but whose
mountains she saw and longed for in her waking dreams.

*I have those stones in my thoughts. I think of their colours, like my
friends – from many Arab and Asian lands.*

*Layla says I have many more friends because people have heard about
what I have done. She tells me there are many others – more than I could
dream of – many women, in many prisons, in many countries.*

*Our crimes are because we are poor.*

She remembers again the translation of the last and final judgement,
the sentence few of them expected – a relief for some, uncalled for by
others.

*They will lash me but I want to be tough. They will not break me just
as he did not break me in the end.*

*I have heard strange stories. People I have never known have helped
my mother and father, have helped me. Strange – helped with the diya, my
blood money, my fine, my release – whatever you call it – helped also with
a scholarship for study. How funny this is. All my life I wanted to study
more. Then no one knew me. I was just one of so many others and still I'm
one of so many others but this time it will not be for me alone. This will be
for all of us somehow.*

*I sit here in the silence, listening to my birds. Maybe they will eat those
cicadas. I like that sound too. It is like water. I sit here listening to the
women somewhere in the distance for there is no one in my area now – poor
and alone – and some stranger offering me money, more than my family
has ever had, just so that I can study afterwards.*

She laughs out loud to herself, more in the irony of the situation than with any bitterness.

*I want to be like Layla. She has worked hard for me. Her spirit has strengthened us. Her brother is in prison too in his own country, fighting for land. Our people have fought for their land too but we need legal people, our own politicians. Our fighters need to see other ways, new ways to get our land back.*

*Here and other places where we fly in search of better lives, for work and for wealth, our people find trouble, our women and other women like us are in jails, locked in homes, in factories, in clubs and bars, in the prisons they build to keep us captive. There are a few who know about us – so many of us. I shall learn about societies and law to rescue people like us from the slaveries which bind us tighter than any rope.*